TWELVE SISTERS

A NOVEL BY

LESLIE
BEATON
HEDLEY

DESERET BOOK COMPANY
SALT LAKE CITY, UTAH

*With love to my first and most enthusiastic editor,
my eternal partner, David Hedley. Without his help,
it would never have come to be.
Always.*

Library of Congress Cataloging-in-Publication Data

Hedley, Leslie Beaton, 1959–
    Twelve sisters : a novel / by Leslie Beaton Hedley.
      p. cm.
    ISBN 0–87579–779–2
    1. Women, Mormon—Canada—Fiction. I. Title.
PS3558.E319T94   1993
813'.54—dc20   93–24540
                                            CIP

Printed in the United States of America

10 9 8 7 6 5 4 3 2

CONTENTS

ACKNOWLEDGMENTS

I wish to express my gratitude to many people:

David, my husband, spent countless hours reading and discussing this book and many more supporting and encouraging me. I give him deepest thanks, as well as my respect and love.

Martine Bates made me believe I could write and challenged me to do so. She nursed several chapters through their infancies, sorting mixed metaphors as she went.

My friend and brother, Shawn Beaton, inspired me to once again open the door of a Mormon meetinghouse. And Judy and Dallas Thompson encouraged me to find a spot for myself in the ward.

Cameron, Alison, and Sean supported me and bragged about me to their friends. I love you, my children. Forever.

The members of the Midnapore Ward, my family, and my circle of friends have encouraged me. I thank them all for their excitement on my behalf. I especially thank Cindy and Don Ady, LaVon Anderson, Margaret Anderson, David Bly, Rob Dudley of the *Herald*, Becky and Drew Galbraith, Rosemarie Horne, Cheri Kennedy of Calgary Medical Services, Phyllis Maher of LDS Social Services, Catherine and Jim Muirhead, Terry Swan, Elin Young, and Toni Young. And thanks to Mom and Dad, too.

My friends at Deseret Book encouraged me and believed in

me. Thanks to them, in particular Suzanne Brady for being a wonderful editor and friend.

This is a work of fiction, although it has its roots in many stories and fragments of stories I have seen and heard. Most of this book really happened only in my head. I hope it is true in the sense that it will encourage readers to look around them with renewed compassion for their sisters (and brothers) in Zion.

CODE 99 AT THE CHAPEL

The radio crackled. "Number Four, what's your location?"

"We're approaching the intersection of Sun Valley Boulevard and Macleod Trail," Cheryl spoke into the microphone she had unclipped from the ceiling. That last call had been a false alarm, an overprotective father panicking after his child's fall from the icy back steps. The child's heavy winter parka had shielded her from the impact. Why the father had called the ambulance when his daughter was standing on her own two feet, rubbing her eyes and screaming, was beyond Cheryl.

"We have a Code Bravo at 14540 Parkland Boulevard," the dispatcher spoke calmly. "Possible cardiac arrest. Assistance is being given at the scene." The paramedics knew the site. It was the Mormon church over by the fire station. "Okay, responding." Cheryl signed off as Jack, driving today, flipped toggle switches on the big console between them, activating the lights and siren. The piercing wail rose into the December sky, announcing their grim mission.

They raced along Macleod Trail, Cheryl's eyes scanning the horizon for cars blocking their way. The street was clogged with holiday shoppers, scrambling to pull over. Sunday afternoon was as bad as Saturday nowadays, Cheryl thought. The ambulance veered from lane to lane, erratically speeding, shifting, sidling, a shining minnow darting along a deep, rock-strewn riverbed.

Traffic lights loomed. There were always some drivers who were too confused or too hurried to move out of the way at an intersection. Cheryl twisted a dial on the console, accelerating the siren's cycle, and cars crouched obediently as the ambulance roared through.

Jack wheeled onto Canyon Meadows Drive, faster now as the ambulance rocketed past manicured lawns and quiet homes toward the church. Cheryl flipped off the siren's insistent wail and looked around her as Jack reached the church parking lot. She assessed the scene.

Small knots of people drifted uneasily around the cars, reaching out toward one another. Wraiths of exhaust spiraled upward in the December chill to the rhythmic thrum of automobile engines. Drivers hesitated and then pulled slowly into the street, snow moaning steadily under the weight of their cars. Round, pale faces pushed up against the windows and stared, wide-eyed, at the ambulance.

Three or four men in suits nodded reassuringly at the occupants of the cars, waving them from the parking lot. Flakes of snow began to sift slowly down upon the men, the bits of icy whiteness falling heavily on their dark shoulders.

"In church!" Cheryl exclaimed. "What a place to have a heart attack!"

The ambulance lights screamed their colors: red-blue, red-blue, red-blue, red-blue, as they scraped the rough brown bricks of the building. The lumbering vehicle, having cleared the curb, crept backward across the asphalt toward the door.

Cheryl jumped from the ambulance before it had reached a

full stop, her arms chilly in the thin uniform shirt of a paramedic. Quickly she threw open the vehicle's side doors and grabbed a large plastic kit and the heart monitor, jamming a clipboard under her arm. Jack ran around to her side and pulled out the oxygen tank and mask.

As Cheryl turned to the confusing scene at the door, she sought a face, a point of reference, to direct her. She spotted a slight, straight woman, clad in a simple, jade green dress, beckoning to her. The woman's countenance was focused, her dark, almond-shaped eyes calm. The paramedic strode up the steps quickly, her partner behind her.

"You're the one who phoned?" Cheryl's breath frosted before her as she spoke. The woman nodded once, her dark hair bobbing slightly. "Which way?" Her voice was tense, not impolite but urgent. At the woman's gesture Cheryl hurtled into the warmth of the church, lugging her gear, followed by the heavy tread of her male partner. She groaned inwardly as people parted before her, their faces ashen. There was a lot of concern here. This person must be well loved. Silent fingers pointed the way down the hall to the double doors. The paramedics' feet, running to the chapel, were muffled thunder. Behind them hurried the light steps of the woman in green.

Cheryl swung back the heavy door and hurried toward the group of people huddled in the open area at the front. A woman's body lay on the floor, another woman hovering over her in the beseeching ritual of CPR. The moment Cheryl's eyes found the victim's face, she put down the useless heart monitor and kit. The lips were distinctly blue. Even as she checked for a pulse, the cool feel of the wrist told Cheryl that there would not be one. The dead woman's visage was as calm and pale as a rock in a deep well, ripples of movement crossing it in time to the ministrations of the woman above her. Small dark patches of blood had begun to pool beneath the woman's skin as she lay, bruising evidence of lividity. The hands were stiff and curled.

The middle-aged woman laboring over the body jerked her gaze toward the paramedics. She had a small, heart-shaped face, with graying blonde hair tousled around it in short curls. Her eyes were shadowed underneath by a soft gray, emphasized by the gray-blue crepe of her dress.

"I'm . . . was . . . a nurse." She turned away again, intent on the figure before her. Thrusting her arms forward, she moved to an age-old rhythm: pounding grain, kneading bread, movements of sustenance and support. "I don't want to break her ribs . . . she's just not that strong . . ." Cheryl gently laid a hand on the nurse's forearm. "It's too late . . . isn't it?" the woman asked anxiously, her eyes searching the paramedic's. Cheryl hesitated only a moment and then nodded slowly. The woman raised her hands to her face, in sorrow or perhaps in prayer. "I guess I knew, but . . ."

The paramedic slowly unclipped the radio from her belt, and stood up. "Dispatch, this is Number Four," she said flatly. The unseen voice responded, brittle in the stillness. "Go ahead, Number Four. What's your status?"

"We have a Code 99. Send the medical examiner." She reached for her clipboard, withdrew a pen from her shirt pocket and began to gently question the woman who still sat by the body, one hand over her mouth, one hand upon the lifeless woman beside her.

Methodically, Cheryl took the information: previous cardiac history, complicating factors, estimated time of death. She realized as she wrote that this one was inevitable; it had been only a matter of time. "As it is for all of us," she thought sadly. The chapel was warm and suddenly oppressive with the visible proof of mortality that lay upon its blue carpet.

Cheryl needed some air; she decided to leave Jack with the body. She picked up the kit and the monitor, meeting the dark eyes of the woman who had shown her in. She walked wordlessly with Cheryl to the heavy wooden doors, opening them for her. "Thanks," she whispered, as the paramedic headed down the silent hallway.

Cheryl exhaled a cloud of frost as she reached into the ambulance and flipped off the lights. She pulled her jacket from the hook inside the vehicle and slipped it on. "I hate Code 99s," she muttered. A woman patted her back, murmuring thanks. The paramedic looked up, surprised, and noticed the people again, their eyes upon her. Shivering, they watched in sorrow and silence as she stowed the gear in the back of the ambulance.

There was nothing to do now but wait for the coroner. Cheryl felt the pack of cigarettes in her pocket and wished she could light one up. She couldn't here, though: it would be . . . out of place.

Cheryl leaned her head back against the cold metal vehicle, wondering if she would ever get used to the empty embrace of death. She zipped up her jacket and hugged herself tightly, trying to warm up.

Welcome!

FOOTHILLS WARD

The Church of Jesus Christ of Latter-day Saints
Bishopric: Glenn B. Malmgren, Bishop
Joseph R. Mercer, First Counselor
Frank L. Klassen, Second Counselor

FAST & TESTIMONY MEETING

Presiding & Conducting: Bishop Glenn B. Malmgren
Opening Hymn: # 220 "Lord, I Would Follow Thee"
Invocation: By invitation
Ward Business: Blessing conferred upon Ethan Bryce Sullivan,
    son of Bryce and Louise Sullivan
Sacrament Hymn: #185 "Reverently and Meekly Now"
Administration of the Sacrament
Bearing of Testimonies
Closing Hymn: #152 "God Be with You Till We Meet Again"
Benediction: By invitation
Chorister: Riko Ikuta
Organist: LaWanda Pilling

ANNOUNCEMENTS

Stake Youth Fireside next Sunday night.
Parkland Stake Center, 7:00 p.m.
For all youth 12 yrs. and up.
Guest speakers: Kent Zobel, Addie Heywood
"Self-Esteem, the Key to Your Future"

!!!CHOIR TODAY!!!

At the home of the Sullivans, 42 Foothills Place.
Call Riko Ikuta for information, 235-2171.

If you wish to place an announcement, please contact Raylene Stone at 235-4782.

RIKO: FROM THE EDGE OF THE FLOCK

Riko Ikuta smoothed her jade green silk dress and pushed the thick curtain of dark hair from her face as she entered the chapel. She hesitated and looked about, her almond-shaped eyes thoughtful. Never had she been so keenly aware of the women in this ward. Never again would she think of the Relief Society as a homogeneous group clustered around a quilting frame. She silently wished she knew at least some of the sisters better. "It would be such a help in my new calling," Riko sighed.

As the ward gathered for the meeting, the women's voices flowed gently in a living current about Riko, underscored by the deep sonority of men's conversation. She witnessed the sharing of small intimacies among the sisters. They were communicating as women often do: interrupting one another, touching one another, gesturing vividly. Riko gently maneuvered her way through the groups of women, trying to be unobtrusive, trying to listen and understand.

"Listen, Tara, don't pressure me." A tense-looking woman addressed her daughter. "I said I would let you know today, and I will." She glanced at her watch as her daughter anxiously grabbed at her hand. "Let's just sit down, okay?" The woman sat and checked her watch again, the way some women compulsively check a mirror.

A tall, russet-haired woman spoke conspiratorially to a friend dressed in a bright turquoise and pink outfit. "Well, Glenda's over there just sick as can be, and she hasn't told a soul. I went over yesterday and took her a casserole . . . You don't suppose she's . . . ?" The speaker hesitated and pulled a soft shawl about her, its warm color matching her hair almost perfectly. "But how are you feeling?" she asked, laying a concerned hand upon the other woman's shoulder. "You look great! I love your new dress!"

The friend smiled. Sister Bertram did look radiant, Riko noted, if somewhat tired. She had a long history of illness, Riko knew. The Bertrams had moved to the city only three months ago. Apparently Sister Bertram had some kind of condition that required them to live near the hospital here. "My husband picked this outfit," Sister Bertram confessed. "I think he's got good taste."

Riko caught a glimpse of her friend Louise, the Primary president, standing several feet inside the chapel. Riko was delighted to recognize the pink stone necklace that Louise wore. It was the one Riko had given her on their trip to California. Louise's infant son Ethan seemed to like the smooth beads as much as Riko did, grabbing at them as his mother spoke. Louise was talking to a large woman who nodded distractedly, holding one of her teenaged daughters in her firm grasp.

"We're just bringing in a new computer listing system. It's wonderful, but what a headache!" Riko turned to see a graceful older woman twisting a heavy gold ring as she spoke. Across from her, a woman with a braided crown of golden hair nodded politely, a smile frozen on her lips. Riko thought the two looked like a picture from the *Ensign*, both so perfectly groomed and lovely. The caption would read something like "sisters share a moment of quiet conversation."

Old Sister Bird was steered to her seat by an officious-looking middle-aged woman, whose mouth was gathered as tightly as her drawstring bag. "Well, I've been worse," Sister Bird opined brightly. "I'm on some new stuff for the arthritis, so we'll see."

A girl of about nine darted around them and was brought up short by the helper's quick hand. "Alison, reverently please," the woman spoke sharply. Judging by the girl's face, the reproof had little, if any, effect.

As the women buzzed, murmured, consoled, and welcomed one another, many kept a wary eye on children. They seemed to be everywhere: carried, dangled, pulled along, in laps or standing on the pews. Riko squeezed one of her hands in the other, experimentally. She wondered what it would be like to hold her own child's hand.

She glanced about the benches. They were littered with bags: diaper bags, purses, tote bags, a few briefcases. Lesson books peeked from some, for Primary or Young Women. Relief Society manuals poked up from others, slips of paper marking the readers' places. There were overstuffed "church" bags, with cloth quiet books, stashes of dry cereal, crayons, and paper—the tools of a peaceful sacrament meeting. Some bags proudly boasted fat wads of diapers, bristling with bottles of juice and teething rings. These bags were cozied in pastel baby blankets, all handmade by someone's grandma or aunt or visiting teacher. There were occasional sleek and elegant handbags, far outnumbered by stretched and aging ones. These veterans of car pools, Safeways, and basketball practices mutely bore testimony to the active lives of their

owners. All lay heavily about the chapel seats, waiting to be lifted
and carried once again on their daily rounds of duty.

Riko's own burdens this day seemed heavy. She wished she
could lay them down on a bench and not take them up again
until some future, undetermined date. She let the current of
voices surround her for a moment and wondered whether it
would buoy her up or pull her under.

These women make life happen all around them. But they
are such a varied group. How on earth will I ever be able to meet
their needs? Riko momentarily closed her stinging eyes. Especially
since I am not really one of them.

Riko felt her cheeks burn as she recalled the number of times
she had not been invited to elders quorum socials or activities.
She was considered a hazard, she supposed, an unattached female.
Nevertheless, she was invited without fail to the high priests'
social functions. Apparently the effects of her fatal charms were
blunted by advanced age and spirituality. Finally Riko had given
up going to ward parties at all. It was easier to be busy that night,
to pretend she did not enjoy dancing. Easier than being asked to
dance as some sort of favor, knowing the request had been
approved by someone's wife.

And the childbirth stories! "Do you know it took me six
hours to dilate the last two centimeters?" one sister had demanded incredulously. Seeing Riko's blank face, she demurred:
"Oh, of course not. How could you?" The sister quickly realized
she was needed somewhere else, as Riko stood rooted to the spot.

Then there were the Cub car pools and basketball schedules
and orthodontic discussions that Riko was not privy to, since she
was not a card- (or picture-) carrying member of the motherhood
club.

And now she, on the fringes of the flock, was being asked to feed them.

Riko sighed and mounted the stairs to the stand. Until they called someone to replace her, she was still the ward chorister. She walked to the wooden board that held the hymn numbers on its polished face. Riko took the plastic cards from the holder and shuffled through them with shaking hands, looking for the right ones, the ones that would tell them all where to look and what to sing. The black and white shapes blurred before her.

If only her new calling were this simple. Why did Sister Gransen have to move? And why oh why did they pick *her* of all people, a single woman, a childless woman, to fill the vacancy left by the capable Sister Gransen?

As Riko fit the trembling cards into their grooves, she recalled the interview with the bishop that led to this flurry of emotion within her.

She had gone to the bishop's office before church last week, as requested. The door was ajar slightly. Riko knocked softly and entered at his quiet reply. Bishop Malmgren was at his desk, his sleeves rolled up, bent over some notes before him.

Riko looked about her. Startled, she recognized the painting on the wall beside Bishop Malmgren as one she had done years before at college. She was surprised he still had it, and faintly embarrassed. It was a typical student painting of the foothills— grain elevators by the railroad tracks, the rising hills behind, the Rocky Mountains in the background. Riko considered it an immature example of her work, formal-looking and unimaginative. Her paintings now were more light-infused, impressionistic. "It really is not my best, Bishop," she said as she gestured toward the wall. "I'll have to do a better one for you."

Bishop Malmgren smiled. "I like this one just fine. Whatever it may lack in originality, it more than makes up for in other ways. It has a sort of . . . whispered potential." He stopped, as if he had been led into saying more than intended. "Please, sit down," he gestured. Riko took the chair opposite the bishop as he reviewed his notes. Pale winter light made the sheer curtains of the office glow behind him.

He looked up. His face was tense as he removed his glasses. He rubbed a hand across his eyes, erasing the lines of concern drawn there, and replaced the glasses. He cleared his throat.

"Sister Ikuta," the bishop began seriously, and then he smiled broadly. "Riko. How long have I known you? I think you were about ten or eleven when I first home taught your family." He paused. "I . . . I heard your grandmother died a few months back. I know you were very close to her. She was a wonderful lady." Riko nodded, her throat tight at the memory of her grandmother's wrinkled face, terrible in its stillness.

The bishop continued. "And your parents, how are they?" He listened attentively while Riko explained that there was not much change, her family was still inactive, still fairly noncommunicative. As she spoke she pictured her mother over the sewing machine, a cigarette in her lips, her dark blonde tendrils curling with the smoke. Still, she conceded, they were planning to get together at Christmas. Riko would drive down to Taber and the little wooden bungalow in a couple of weeks.

Riko listened to the bishop's earnest reply, wondering silently what the real reason was for her being there. Surely this wasn't just a family checkup. The discussion moved to Riko's life in general: work, relationships, her current calling, tithing—Riko began to get nervous. Bishop Malmgren was leaning forward in his chair now, talking about the Gransens, as Riko's mind flew about for a mental image of the family. Gransen—wait! Sister Gransen was . . .

" . . . Relief Society president," intoned the bishop, arriving with Riko at her conclusion. "We have inquired of the Lord. We know you'd make a fine Relief Society president, Sister Ikuta."

Riko could not speak at first. Me? This must be a mistake. But Bishop Malmgren looked steadily at her, the overhead light gleaming from his steel-rimmed glasses. "I know this might be kind of . . . a surprise."

A surprise? She couldn't have been more startled if his proposal had been one of marriage. "Bishop, are you sure?" was all she could manage. "There are so many women in this ward—very capable, experienced women . . ."

"Experience gained through service. As you will gain it, Sister Ikuta," was his reply. "Would you think about it, Riko? You're compassionate, intelligent—I know you give one hundred percent of your effort to whatever you take on. And I'm certain your spiritual health is very good." He paused, studying the painting on his wall for a moment, and then turned to look directly into Riko's eyes.

"It is a job that calls, above all, for spirituality—for compassion and sensitivity. We need someone who will really help the sisters 'come unto Christ'."

Riko shook her head slightly in disbelief. "With all respect, Bishop, I am hardly a stellar example of Latter-day Saint womanhood," she replied, finding her voice at last. "I don't think I would be much of a Relief Society president." Riko wondered if this were really happening. They couldn't possibly want her. But it seemed they did. When the bishop did not reply, Riko added, "I mean, I am not compassionate enough. I can be very impatient. I'm a career woman, a graphic artist. I don't even have a family . . . not like almost all of the other sisters in the ward." She hesitated and then decided to name her biggest objection. "I don't fit in, Bishop. I am not really . . . one of them."

The bishop angled his head to one side and narrowed his eyes. He seemed to search the air above Riko's head for his next words. At last he looked into her face again. "You are a worthy sister in the Church of Jesus Christ. I have seen evidence of your commitment and compassion over many years. I think," he added, "that you are much more suited to this calling than you can see at the moment." He paused and leaned forward, still fixing her with his gaze. "I know," he said simply, "that you're the one. What I'm asking, Riko, is that you think about it, that you pray for an understanding of the Lord's wishes in this matter. I'll talk to you in a couple of days. I know you'll know what to do."

The bishop beamed at her once more and stood, the signal for her to rise. They shook hands, and Riko turned on quaking legs to leave. As she reached the door he spoke again.

"Riko, few people are completely ready for a calling when they receive it. But you grow in it, in ways you never dreamed possible." Riko nodded dumbly, still trying to grasp the situation and wrestle it into reality.

Grow? Riko thought as she slid the last number into place. She had no doubt she would grow. But in what way? Grow older? Grow slowly crazy? Grow more certain of her own ineptitude? Grow even more distant from the women she was supposed to lead? Grow . . . She had a sudden mental picture. Riko smiled her wide, slow smile and pushed back her hair once more. Perhaps she would grow another Riko so she could go through the world two by two, like everyone else in the Church. They would be joined at the hip, as Riko had teased her friend Louise that she and her husband, Bryce, were.

The smile faded as Riko's thoughts became serious again. It had taken a while to receive the answer the bishop was so sure of. She had begun her fast immediately: reading, praying, thinking. Over and over again she came up empty. Yet the bishop was so sure of her. "I wish I had his confidence," she murmured, as she pulled on her heavy parka in preparation for a walk by herself in the winter twilight. Riko strolled aimlessly around the suburb at first and then took the sidewalk that ran along the rim of Fish Creek Park. Here she could see the dark abyss of the ravine below her, untouched by the colored lights that proclaimed Christmas from the other side. She studied the sky. This grand color-wash could never be duplicated on a computer screen. Still, out of long habit, she estimated the percentages of color saturation, from the inky black heights to the paler, softer twilight.

The evergreens drooped slightly, gracefully, under their blue-white burdens. Riko snapped a twig underfoot and brooded. I don't know anyone who's ever been in the presidency who wasn't at least married. She enumerated her faults: I don't like to talk to people I don't know well. I don't see most of these women socially. I don't know how to knit or crochet or even sew a straight line.

The phrase evoked a painful memory. Riko winced, recalling her mother's angry face. She waved a seam ripper in angry strokes over Riko's head. Riko's seventh-grade home ec project lay crumpled on the table. "Your sister can at least sew a straight line, for pity's sake! Get your head out of the clouds and pay attention. You think you're so smart—well, you're not! Just follow instructions for a change!"

Riko kicked the snow as she walked, watching skiffs plume upward from her black boots. Her eyes followed the sparkling crystals and then stopped.

The deer stood about six feet from her, turning its full, deep gaze upon her. The doe was beautiful. She carried herself proudly, her head high. Her nose was a dark patch of velvet. She wore the fur of her throat and shoulders as a queen wears her mantle of royalty. She contemplated Riko, including her in her pristine world. Riko felt as if she had stepped into a sacred place, touched with the silver threads of a parting veil. The tumult in her heart ceased. She stood stock-still, marveling at the majesty of the animal before her. There was no room within her for anything other than the sight and silence and awe of this moment.

The doe tentatively stepped forward and then continued on her way, crossing the street under the glare of streetlights and slipping into shadows. Riko stared after the deer. At first she didn't see the others. Silent shapes now joined the first doe, delicate feet picking their way across the street to the leader's side. Riko merely watched, not moving, for many minutes. Her breath hung before her, a warm vapor surrounding her face in the cold night. The deer moved slowly, melting into the blackness of a quiet side street. Still Riko stood, fixed under the streetlight's bright lens.

At last the cold penetrated her thin boots and gloves, and Riko knew she must move onward. Slowly she resumed her walk, dazed as if she had seen a vision.

The bishop was right, she realized: she should take this calling. Wrapped, shivering, in the night's magic, Riko felt again a sense of wonder at the doe's deep gaze, watched once more the group of deer as they followed one another into the darkness, gliding one after the other like drops melting from a branch.

It felt right, now.

When she reached home, Riko knelt just inside the doorway in the icy puddles left there by her feet. Her hot tears fell as she accepted the calling in prayer and pleaded for help to do it well.

"If I could just sense their needs, help them in some way . . ." she whispered.

Even before Bishop Malmgren phoned her, Riko began the process of choosing her counselors and secretary. The decisions were difficult ones. She didn't know the women in her ward well. She knew she must open herself to the Spirit fully, as she had no other criteria to guide her.

The ward list lay in front of Riko on her drafting table. "Let's see. Ady, Allred, Anderson . . . not Lenora Bertram—her health is so poor. Same goes for Esther Bird—she's earned a rest." Riko continued to scan the names: "Bly, Bohne, Boynton. Ruth Boynton? Maybe . . . Byam, Cahoon, Carson, Daines . . . no, Andrea isn't a member yet . . . Duce, Evans, Fairbanks . . . " Then she came across a name that leapt out at her. "Rhonda Fitzpatrick." Rhonda was the most capable person Riko knew, the woman you phoned if you needed a ride to the hospital, pronto, with no hysterics. Riko wrote this one down on a pad at her side and resumed reading. "Galbraith, Harding, Jensen . . . " Glenda Klassen would be perfect . . . good with people, upbeat, and organized. But she had a lot of children, and her husband was in the bishopric. Riko read on, jotted down another name, and turned back to the ward list. "Malmgren, Mercer, Muirhead, Nalder, Noames, Petraski, Pilling, Rasmussen." Sharon Rasmussen was a possibility. Riko noted the name. "Redfern, Sanderson, Stone . . . Louise Sullivan." Again Riko paused. The only woman in the ward she knew well was Louise. But Louise was Primary president already and loving it. No, not Louise. "Virginia Thorne?" Virginia seemed aloof, but perhaps she was really just shy, as Riko herself was. Riko was doubtful. She pictured Virginia and that mane of golden hair. *Shy* was not a word that came to mind. Still, she should be considered. She wrote Virginia's name carefully on the paper and pored over the rest of the ward list. When she had finished, after the Youngs and the Zatylnys, Riko went over her handwritten list repeatedly, pondering, praying, deliberating, and listening.

It had taken four more days to choose the presidency. Over and over she had prayed for confirmation of her choices, and over and over she was reassured. The sensation of asking and being answered repeatedly made Riko feel like a child who keeps tip-toeing into her parents' room at night to see if they're still there. The answers didn't change. Always, patient. Always, the same.

Riko turned from the now ready hymn numbers and walked toward her seat just as the bishop sat down near her and gave her a knowing smile. He would present her name and those of her presidency today for the sustaining vote of ward members.

What would be going through everyone's mind as she stood up here on the stand watching them raise their arms to the square in approval? Or perhaps disapproval?

Riko knew. "A single woman as Relief Society president?" would be the reaction of many, probably most. They would be as incredulous as she had been. It was impossible to be more so.

Would they accept her as Relief Society president? She had never seen anyone not sustained. And she had prayed; she was the right one. At least, I'm pretty sure, she thought uneasily. But will *they* think I'm the right one?

Riko's restless thoughts returned to the task at hand. Who will they get to be the chorister? This ward has a definite shortage of musical talent.

She sat down and began to flip through the hymnbook, care-fully marking her places.

Riko glanced up for a moment as a woman entered uncer-tainly from the foyer and stood a few feet from the door.

Something about her held Riko's attention. It was true she didn't know some of the sisters very well, but this woman . . . Riko was sure she'd never seen her before. The woman was gazing raptly around her now. Spiky hair and big earrings . . . she didn't look like any of the sisters Riko had met. And yet she had kids in tow. But no, her husband was decidedly ill at ease. They must be investigators, she decided.

Riko made a mental note to inquire about the new family. Great. I'm not even sustained, and here I am nosing into everyone's business, she smiled wryly. Next I'll be rushing covered dishes all over the south end of the city. Riko pictured herself, casserole in hand, on a doorstep in the middle of winter. The sister behind the door—would she be happy to see Riko? Or would she be stiff and polite, not inviting her beyond the entranceway?

Unobtrusively, Riko bowed her head and prayed. Would she be allowed in? She could almost feel the warm dish in her hand, the cold air around her, as she waited.

MAGGIE:
TESTING THE WATERS

Maggie Hartley squared her shoulders under the straps of her heavy bag. This is it, she thought. This is what I have been dreading and wanting and fighting. I'm going to look out of place, I'm going to feel out of place, but I told Cam I was going to do it, and I darned well am. Sliding the diaper bag up, clutching the baby, she reached for the heavy door.

Maggie paused as she entered the building. She had never been here before, and yet it was eerily familiar to her. The angle of the light, the way it diffused softly about the foyer, the faces of the people, muted organ music drifting from the chapel. It was unknown and yet known. This place echoed from a distant memory.

Cam walked in just behind her. He stood awkwardly. He had come reluctantly, "to prove you are wrong," he had said in his usual, tactful-as-a-sledgehammer way. Cam didn't own a suit, and Maggie realized that marked him as an outsider here. That and the absence of any clothing beneath his white shirt. Maggie hurriedly checked her own attire. It was conservative, for her. Basic dress and jacket, pumps, and a handbag. The wild earrings, though—she knew they were sure to stand out. And her spiky hairstyle. She could only compromise so much, she told herself.

An air of unreality seemed to hang about Maggie this afternoon. From the time she had awakened this morning, she had known that this was the day, that she was finally going to do it. Maggie didn't care if every Mormon in the city gawked at her. She was going to go back to church.

The baby on her hip and her daughter in hand, Maggie began to cross the foyer. It was exciting to be back at last, but nerve-racking, too. She must try to be objective about this experience, she told herself, to weigh the options carefully. When she looked into her heart, though, she knew the decision had already been made, weeks ago. Her breath was coming quickly. She could feel her pulse in her throat. Maggie hoped no one would ask her why she was here. Perhaps their little family would pass unnoticed among all these people? If she had to talk out loud about it, her voice would probably shake and, well, it would sound so corny, Maggie thought. The prodigal daughter.

Why exactly was she here? What had brought her back to church? Maggie tried to find one reason, to find a simple answer. She hadn't set foot in a Mormon church for twelve years. Into the interval she had packed a lot of living, much of it in conflict with the things she had been taught in Mutual. Cam had fallen in love with a headstrong girl who described herself as an ex-Mormon, a girl who spoke her own mind and didn't like to fit into the molds others cast.

"Come on, Bethany, come with Mommy," Maggie coaxed as her daughter paused to lock eyes with another toddler.

Now that headstrong "ex-Mormon" was balancing a bag full of diapers, bottles, rattles, and toy cars on one hip and a baby on the other. Bethany straggled along behind. Cam, with four-year-old Alex, followed. Both looked equally uncomfortable.

There had been a Feeling, Maggie knew. That strange and peaceful feeling she used to get when she knew that everything was okay. She still got The Feeling, sometimes. When she and Cam hiked in the Rockies, for instance. Or on cold winter mornings when the house lay sleeping under a snowy blanket, the furnace purring, and she alone was awake. Then she would savor the small home, her children, and her sleeping husband, and tears would come to her eyes. The Feeling was . . . being so full she could hardly contain it.

She used to have that feeling a lot more often. She remembered that.

"The Mormons!" Cam had been incredulous. "They're chauvinists! How could you even think of going back there after all you told me about them?" There followed several days of negotiations and outright arguments. "Why don't we just go to the Church of the Redeemer down the street? What does it really matter? One church is the same as another. What counts is giving our kids something to hold on to." Maggie saw that Cam refused to view the LDS Church as anything but a bunch of fundamentalist hard-liners.

Well, thought Maggie, he may be right about that. But you have to be passionate about what you believe.

Yesterday she had finally shown him her patriarchal blessing, dug out from underneath the old letters and dried flowers in a musty box. Cam remained skeptical, but when he looked at Maggie's face, his expression softened. Reluctantly, he agreed to go with her.

It seemed a long walk across the church foyer to the chapel doors. Maggie imagined that the foyer had been pumped full of honey, and she was dragging her unwilling feet through hazy golden dimness to the doors. A woman's voice piped up beside her.

"Hello, I don't believe we've met." The woman was petite and blonde, swathed in delicate blue-gray crepe. She smiled sweetly. Perky, thought Maggie. Mormon women are so relentlessly perky.

"Hello," Maggie smiled uncertainly. "My name's Maggie, and this is my husband, Cam." Cam made a halfhearted attempt at a smile.

"Well, hi there! I'm Glenda Klassen." The woman's bright blue eyes were betrayed by soft shadows beneath them. She shifted the baby on her hip and then added, "Are you investigators?"

Now there was a phrase Maggie hadn't heard in a long time. It reminded her of Nancy Drew mysteries. "Uh, sort of. I used to be a member, when I was a teenager."

Great, Maggie thought. Now Glinda the Good Witch, or whatever her name is, will tell the whole Relief Society, and they'll be on me in a flash with their knitting needles poised. So much for slipping into the fold quietly.

"Well, then I guess you *are* investigators!" Perky bubbled. She really seemed very nice. Maggie made up her mind to be more forgiving. She was here for a new start, after all. "If you have any questions or anything, just call me any time," Glenda continued. "It's nice to meet you! I sure hope we see you again!" She waved over her shoulder as she attempted to round up several children and herd them into the chapel.

A heavy hand landed on Cam's shoulder. A voice boomed, "Welcome! Glad to have you here. Where you from?" A stocky man, with eyes that were nearly matched in brilliance by the blue of his tie, smiled broadly.

Taking his cue from the previous conversation, Maggie supposed, Cam replied hesitantly. "Uh. We're. Investigators. I guess." Cam looked as if he would rather be anywhere but in a Mormon church.

The man laughed, an act that seemed to engage his entire face and several inches of his balding scalp. Presently he took a more sober aspect, and giving Cam's shoulder an avuncular squeeze, he boomed once more. "Well, come on in, kids—the water's fine!" His features broke formation hastily, reforming themselves into what appeared to be habitual jocularity. Then, winking, the boomer turned and headed into the meeting. A smiling, roundish woman with fluffy, pale blonde hair trotted at his side.

Although smiling, Maggie cringed inwardly. What must Cam think of these people? His own family was so undemonstrative, so quiet. The Personal Space Family, Maggie called them sarcastically. Cam did not usually deal well with this type of sudden familiarity.

Maggie stole a glance at her husband. He seemed all right. He did look slightly pained, but at least he hadn't turned around and headed for the car. They were stopped again at the door to the chapel, given a ward bulletin, and greeted warmly. They replied politely and nervously shook the offered hands.

After entering the chapel, Maggie and Cam hesitated a few feet from the door. Then Cam headed toward a half-empty row. Maggie simply stood for several moments, absorbing the room around her. She had become suddenly unaware of Cam and of the child she held in her arms.

The layout of the chapel was like all the other LDS chapels Maggie could recall: lots of horizontal lines, little ornamentation except for a basket of flowers near the microphone, fluorescent

light angled against the brick backdrop of the far wall. The chapel
was filling up quickly. Organ music played softly, a hymn she
vaguely remembered. A dark-haired woman sat up at the front, in
what Maggie had always thought of as the speakers' seats. For a
moment the woman's eyes held Maggie's. People hummed about;
chatting, finding places to sit. It was an unremarkable sight. Yet
Maggie was transfixed. It was as if the very air held a quality that
she had needed and not breathed for years. She felt charged with
electricity as she stood dumbstruck in the aisle, soaking it in, one
thought running through her mind: There it is again! The
Feeling.

Maggie suddenly felt foolish and very vulnerable standing
there alone. She collected herself and found Cam's anxious
glance. Holding her baby closer to conceal her slight tremble,
Maggie moved to sit with him. As she did so, she felt as if every
eye in the congregation was upon them.

She fervently hoped Cam would understand. She had to
come. She just had to. She could ignore her conscience no longer. Thoughts that had been long buried continued to surface.
She wanted stability. She wanted a sense of belonging, of com-
munity. And she wanted spirituality. Her life was missing an
entire dimension that she knew existed, because she had once
experienced it. It was something like having The Feeling, only
it was more sustained. Maggie had tried every way she had known
to get that quality of peace and strength back again, every way
but the one that she knew would work. At last, defeated, she had
brought the family all here.

Once seated, she looked about her. This ward was smaller
than her old one. She drew comfort from the familiar yet strange
surroundings.

She picked out Boomer and his wife Fluffy, and there was

Perky looking decidedly less perky with a row of kids beside her. There was real variety in this ward, she noted. She saw a lovely, graceful woman with a crown of braided blonde hair and a face like a china doll. She had a little girl beside her, perhaps her daughter. Children were everywhere. Some of the members looked tired, as if their lives had been thrown in the wash one time too many, like the big woman with the red-blonde hair. Some looked genuinely happy to be there. Some were poised; some, relaxed. Many smiled, seeming mildly curious about why Cam and Maggie and their children were there.

It shouldn't be too hard to find a place here, Maggie thought. To build a foundation for the children among these solid-looking people. Cam, Maggie noticed, was playing with his tie, shuffling his feet on the blue carpet. But only if we decide we want to, of course, she added uncertainly.

A man stood and began speaking into the microphone. Maggie wondered if he was the bishop. The organ sounded once more. The dark-haired, graceful woman Maggie had seen earlier stood at the front in a lovely green dress. Her arms were raised like petals. She looked to Maggie as if she were poised to dance. The chorister's eyebrows lifted, and she smiled and moved her arms in large, slow movements as she led the opening hymn. Maggie thought she looked for all the world as if the salvation of this ward depended on her sincerity as a chorister.

The hymn was only faintly familiar to Maggie, which was a letdown. She would have liked to sing out, so as not to disappoint the music leader. And Maggie wanted to show these curious people that she belonged here.

During the prayer she cracked open one eye to look at Cam. His family was very down on organized religion. Yet here he was with his head bowed and his eyes closed. Did he hate this?

Maggie wondered. In any case, he was sure to have lots to say to her when they got in the car. Maybe he'd never come back again. She hoped he would.

The invocation itself did not seem unusual to Maggie, from what she remembered of past ones. The sincerity of the sister praying impressed her, however. Perhaps that would impress Cam too, she thought hopefully, and maybe he would come back next week. They could get the kids started in Primary . . . Maggie's happy thoughts screeched to a halt at the word testimonies.

She looked at the bulletin in her hand. Oh no! Today is fast and testimony Sunday! Why oh why did I pick this Sunday to come! Cam is going to totally hate this! She sat stiffly, dreading Cam's reaction. There was nothing to do now but hope for the best.

Maggie remembered clearly now how babies were blessed. She watched as brothers came from the congregation and took their places. The burly man with the squirming baby went up first. Then others joined him. The men stood in a circle around the hidden child, their hands on one another's shoulders. To Maggie, it seemed like a circle of love and protection. A few rows ahead, she could see the baby's mother holding herself, blinking back tears.

Now that she had children herself, Maggie thought she could better understand the priesthood ordinance of a baby's blessing. It had once seemed to her a male ritual, but now she realized that she'd misunderstood. This was a special time of bonding between father and child, a bestowal. It was a way for the father to bring the spiritual to the physical, the being created within the mother's womb.

With a deep, resonant voice, the father poured out a blessing of love, protection, goodness, upon the head of his son. The father's words occasionally caught in his throat, checked by his intense happiness. He was grateful, so grateful for this child. Cam could identify with that, she thought. He was a loving father. Maggie glanced at her husband. He was listening intently.

Maggie closed her eyes again and imagined the father's arms around the wriggling body of his son and the hands of the others buoying the child up. A thrill ran through her. She felt privileged to be here. She blinked rapidly when the blessing was finished, glad to flip through the hymnbook to disguise her emotion.

Maggie's voice swam through the hymn awkwardly, clutching at remembered notes and phrases. It was like looking at an old photograph of herself or trying on a dress she had worn years ago and loved. It felt strange, but she was somehow compelled to do it and drew wistful comfort from the act.

She had not really thought about the sacrament for a long, long time. Years ago, she had taken it every Sunday, almost automatically. It was just something that Mormons did, Maggie had felt, before the real business of the meeting, the talks. Now, as Maggie looked at the snowy tablecloth and the young men surrounding it at the front of the chapel, she tried to recall the sacrament more clearly. Bread and water, representing Christ's sacrifice for mankind, for us, she remembered. This was going to throw Cam for a loop, Maggie knew. Never in his thirty-one years had he experienced anything like it. Talk about organized religion! she thought, as she worried about Cam's response to the sacrament prayer. But it was her own response she was not prepared for.

She gasped inaudibly as the young man intoned, *"O God, the Eternal Father, we ask thee in the name of thy Son, Jesus Christ . . . "*

It was as if a voice inside Maggie whispered, "What took you so long?"

Her eyes flew open. At the front of the chapel, a young man was humbly kneeling before a lace-covered table. His face was tense with concentration as he prayed over the bits of bread before him. The dim light from outside brushed his face as he spoke the well-worn syllables of the prayer, the prayer that Maggie had thought forgotten but found lingering in the recesses of her mind. As she listened, she felt as if she were hearing a favorite, beloved verse from long ago.

" . . . *to bless and sanctify this bread to the souls of all those who partake of it . . . "*

She closed her eyes once more and saw a long, echoing hallway lined with the unopened doors of possibility. Maggie knew she had denied this homecoming for many years, had paced up and down as the sound of her steps ricocheted about her, going nowhere. She had been looking for something else, perhaps. Distracted, or just avoiding; never quite seeing, never opening the door that would lead her back here.

The words of the prayer resonated in her heart. She knew them, believed them, wanted them to be true. She wanted the familiar arms of the Church to hold her and accept her as its own. That's why she had come here, she admitted. She had known it all along. For Cam's sake and for the sake of her pride, she'd pretended she was just testing the waters. But she had known.

" . . . *that they may eat in remembrance of the body of thy Son, and witness unto thee, O God, the Eternal Father . . . "*

Maggie was overcome with the desire to put off the old hurts and doubts and anger. It had been so long ago and so superficial. She wanted desperately just to dive into activity with her children. She wanted to hear all the familiar hymns and see her children go to Primary. She wanted to see her husband baptize them and the family to go to church together each Sunday. The words of prayer called her back. Called her, and her family, to start anew.

Being different suddenly didn't matter so much any more. Being a sister, being part of this, did.

Her past words came back to mock her. "The Church is for white men, by white men." Tears sprang to Maggie's eyes and her face suddenly felt very warm. She felt ashamed, like a child caught telling a lie. She was conscious that she hadn't really tried to find out the reasons behind much of the doctrine. She hugged herself with her folded arms. It's not for me! she recalled her stubborn vow.

But oh, yes. Yes it was.

She would read, find answers this time. She took a deep, calming breath. She must hold herself in, be cautious. She could not jump in all at once. It was too big a leap to make without her husband. But oh! she agonized silently, What if he won't jump with me?

" . . . *that they are willing to take upon them the name of thy Son . . .* "

She remembered women she had known years ago, the ones whose husbands were not members. Those women had valiantly attended church every Sunday. They struggled to keep their children righteous without benefit of the priesthood in their homes. She did not want to be one of those women. She wanted it all.

" . . . *and keep his commandments which he has given them . . .* "

Maggie's thoughts ran on. What would it be like to be a Mormon matron? She'd have to cut out coffee. A bubble of giddiness surfaced; she'd wear wild Bermuda shorts in the summer and eat Jell-O salad and drive a minivan! She smiled to herself. It would be worth it.

" . . . *always have his Spirit to be with them* . . . "

The Feeling, the Spirit! Maggie struggled with her emotions. To always have it with her! Oh, dear God, she prayed. If it can only happen!

" . . . *Amen.*"

Maggie was relieved to see that Cam didn't partake of the bread as it was passed; she knew that he should not. But what about me? She hesitated. Maggie felt the smooth, warm handle, the heavy tray's weight as she deliberated. Small white pieces of bread, their torn edges reminding Maggie of bits of tissue paper, lay in readiness for hands to claim them. They are so white! Maggie thought, gazing at her own hand holding the tray.

She passed it on. She could not. She felt unworthy.

She wondered how many pairs of eyes had watched that silent decision.

Maggie held her breath. There was a long way to go. She turned to look at her husband, holding their little daughter on his lap. He looked more relaxed now, as he cradled Bethany. She loved Cam so much! Could he ever possibly investigate the Church, let alone join it? Anxiously, she tried to catch his eye, to magically divine his thoughts. But he remained deep in contemplation, withdrawn from her in his assessment.

As she prepared for the second sacrament blessing, Boomer's voice seemed to ring joyously in her ears: "Well, come on in, kids—the water's fine!"

Maggie bit her lip. She was waist-deep already. She bowed her head.

"*O God, the Eternal Father* . . . "

RUTH:
A MOTHER KNOWS

Ruth Boynton was a plump woman, scrubbed and shiny in her Sunday clothes. Ordinarily, she did not rest heavily in the pew, as so many overweight women do, but seemed to perch, a large pink balloon about to float away. This resemblance was due not only to her rosy skin but also to her nervous habit of bobbing slightly in agreement with the speaker's words. More than once a neophyte deacon had mistakenly started toward her, microphone in hand, in response to Ruth's enthusiastic movement.

Today, Ruth Boynton's broad shoulders sagged beneath her wide Battenberg lace collar. She felt as if the air were slowly leaking out of her. As if to augment that process, Ruth sighed, fluttering the order of service in her hand. She was dimly aware that a baby was being blessed and dutifully looked to the front of the chapel, her thoughts drifting.

Darla had come back from BYU. And that was a problem.

Darla was Ruth and Ted Boynton's eldest daughter: nineteen, leggy, and smart, the kind of girl everyone else told them was wonderful. The kind of girl who could impress her Laurel adviser with a values project in the afternoon and have her parents up all that night waiting for her, her mother furious and pacing, her father's face pinched with worry.

"Something is wrong, Mom," Darla's voice had quavered over the phone. "Something really bad, and I have to come home. I want to tell you in person."

Ruth's flesh prickled at her daughter's words. "Honey, you're not . . ." Ruth paused and then sighed. No, it couldn't be. "Are you eating enough? Are you sick?"

Darla's nervous laugh crackled in her mother's ear. "We'll talk when I get home, okay? Don't worry."

But Ruth had worried. For two hours after Darla's call, she tried to simply accept her daughter's decision not to talk about it. Ruth paced the house, picking up stray items and loudly calling the owners to put them away. Then she scrubbed the kitchen floor, although she had done it only the day before. Finally, she stalked over to the telephone desk, saying loudly, "It's about time someone went through this stack of mail." That was a quick task. And then she was left sitting at the desk, staring at the telephone. Darla's number was on the list taped to the wall in front of her. Ruth dialed quickly, telling herself that she had the right to know and that her own daughter should not keep secrets from her.

The girl who answered was not sure where Darla was. She sounded very vague and unimpressed by Ruth's urgency. Finally she agreed to go look. Ruth fumed as the minutes ticked by, imagining how much she was paying for the call. At last Darla picked up the phone. "Mom?"

"Darla, this is ridiculous. You have to tell me what's going on."

"Look, I've told you all I can tell you right now." She lowered her voice. "I can't talk here, all right?"

"Where, then? Tell me where you can talk, and I'll phone you there."

There was a loud sigh from Darla. "No. I'll be home in three days. I'll see you then." The phone clicked, and the line went dead. "This is unconscionable!" Ruth muttered. "Hanging up on her mother. She is going to hear about that!"

Darla was "not home" to Ruth's subsequent phone calls. Ruth had been forced to accept the fact that she would have to wait for her daughter's news.

Ruth meticulously prepared Darla's peach and green room. Darla must feel comfortable in her home. It was to be a safe haven. Ruth took down the ruffled priscilla curtains and washed and ironed them, hanging them carefully so that they were evenly gathered. She made up the bed with crisp, cool new sheets, and in the center, against the puffy pillow in its sham, she set Darla's oldest, most loved, stuffed bear. She bought Darla's favorite shampoo and soap for the linen cupboard and put sachets in the closet and drawers.

The family all tried hard to be happy at Darla's return. Janeen, a year and a half younger than Darla, became thoughtful, almost pensive. Janeen and Darla had shared their own world when they were younger. Ruth had boasted that there never had been two sisters closer to each other. Yet in recent years, Janeen had borne the brunt of Darla's adolescent anger. Ruth reflected that Darla had developed a nasty way of turning on those closest to her.

She shook her head. The news that Darla was dropping out of school had hit like a bombshell. Darla had worked so hard for that scholarship. It was inconceivable that she was throwing such a good chance away. A storm of angry disbelief rained down upon Ted's dark head from his voluble wife. "She can't leave school. We can't let her, Ted. She is ruining her life! Ted!" Ruth's flushed face, like a closed fist, thrust itself in front of him. Shaking her head, she resumed her staccato walk across his study.

Ted sat immobile in his leather wing chair, watching his wife pace the small room like a trapped lioness, waiting. As always, once Ruth's fury was spent, her voice hoarse, her arms limp at her sides—when she had sunk onto the sofa—he spoke. His voice was low; his words, precise.

"There's no use being angry when we don't even know what the problem is. I think we should be calm. We should pray about this and wait to see what she has to say for herself. I'm sure what-ever it is can be overcome." He and Ruth stared wordlessly at one another, reading the expressions on each other's faces: Ruth's tearstained and red, Ted's lined and somber. At last Ted picked up the newspaper and opened it briskly.

Ruth left the room silently. She told herself to breathe deeply. She told herself that Ted was right. They must be calm and unit-ed in support of Darla. They should just go about their normal lives. Darla needed that more than anything else right now. They would let her tell them in her own way.

Darla had been home for nearly a week, and still there had been little communication from the Boyntons' bright, cover-girl-pretty daughter. The rest of the family did chores, went to school or work, chatted on the phone; Ruth waited anxiously, her thoughts never far from Darla. But it seemed Darla had come home only to hide in the bedroom that Ruth had so carefully pre-pared. The room that was now a jumble of clothing and makeup and discarded candy bar wrappers. When she emerged, it was for meals, to use the bathroom, or to go out for a run in Fish Creek

Park. Ruth began to question her about her life at college, hoping to glean clues to Darla's unspoken problem. The effect of her scrutiny was to push her daughter further from her, heightening Ruth's frustration.

Ruth shifted in her seat. Bryce Sullivan, short and dark-haired, carried his newly blessed son to his wife's anxious arms. The couple sat gazing at the child as if he were the only thing that mattered. Boys are easier, Ruth thought grimly, as she watched the boy happily chomping his fist.

Dinner Monday night, Darla's first night home, was to have been special. Ruth had prepared her oldest daughter's favorite foods to welcome her home, to show that no matter what, they still loved her. Beef stroganoff with sour cream, baby carrots in a buttery ginger sauce, Caesar salad, and dark chocolate cake for dessert. Janeen had set the table silently, her thoughts clouded behind lowered eyes.

Darla surveyed the dining room with obvious delight. "Mom, it's beautiful!" Ruth smiled at her daughter's reaction, her hand on Darla's back, and let her own gaze scan the room once more, pleased with her efforts. The small chandelier had been dimmed to a warm ivory glow that was reflected from the gleaming china. ("Royal Albert Fine Bone China, Memory Lane" the stamp on the underside of each piece proudly proclaimed.) There were cloth napkins to match the pale blue tablecloth and crystal salt and pepper shakers. Every hint of tarnish on the silver had been eliminated by Ruth's determined hand.

Against the wall stood a lighted cabinet. The glass shelves held trophies and awards for academic achievement given to the Boynton children, alongside the glossy ribbons Darla had earned in track and field. The latest addition to the cabinet gleamed from the top shelf. It was a plaque which boasted, in engraved script: "Darla R. Boynton, Valedictorian, Lord Beaverbrook High School, 1992."

As guest of honor, Darla was asked to say the blessing. Ruth then bustled to the kitchen and returned with the stroganoff, which she set upon the table. "I hope you like it!" she chirped, smiling as she removed the lid with a potholder. Fragrant steam teased the family's nostrils.

"I thought you would have made burritos, Mom. I've been dying for them," Darla said innocently. Anger flared within Ruth. Her grip on the heavy glass lid tightened. Darla saw her mother's firm mouth and smiled charmingly. "But I'm so glad you made this," she added. "It smells wonderful. And it's my *second* favorite meal!" Ted's dark eyes found Ruth's and sent a message: calm, calm.

Whether or not the meal was Darla's favorite, it seemed she couldn't get enough of it. Ruth began to relax as she noted the family's obvious enjoyment. "Mom, this is so much better than the cafeteria food down there. You would not believe the stuff they serve. Well, some of it's okay, I guess. But there's nothing to compare with this!"

Darla then chatted amiably, remembering to ask Kevin about his birthday. She told them about her friends, clothes, firesides. They all smiled. Darla was acting remarkably calm, instead of unleashing the shrill tirades they had expected. Darla even complimented Janeen on her new earrings. Under the glow of the chandelier, Ruth and Janeen exchanged a glance, Janeen startled, Ruth pleased. There was the clinking of silver on china, the dull sound of glasses on a covered table, occasional laughter in the easy conversation. Darla ate every bit of her food, Ruth noted with pride. There's nothing like home cooking, she told herself, as she rose for another trip to the kitchen. Ruth served the cake triumphantly, giving Darla the first piece, noting the effect of the low light on Darla's sculpted cheekbones.

Ruth sighed. "I had cheekbones like that once," she said admiringly. She laughed. "Until I had you!" Indeed, Ruth had the photos to prove it. She had often shown the girls: summer cabin photos, prom photos, wedding photos, all of Ruth in size five bathing suits and gowns that emphasized the tiny waist. Her eyes had been large and luminous on her small round face, her thick red-gold hair had tumbled down her back. Ruth motioned for perhaps the thousandth time to the wedding photo of her and Ted that hung on the wall nearby. "Would you believe I had . . . "

" . . . a twenty-two-inch waist." Darla finished her mother's sentence and smiled archly over a glass of milk. "Yes. And then you got pregnant with me. I know."

The gentle clinking stopped. Ted cleared his throat and turned the talk to Darla's studies. Ruth could see where Ted was trying to steer the conversation. Darla once again chose to be evasive, not rising to the bait of Ted's indirect questioning.

Ruth, always more forthright than her husband, decided to take matters in hand. As she cleared the dessert dishes, she spoke to the youngest children. "Kevin, Megan, you're excused from dishes tonight. You may leave the table." The surprised children needed no prodding. They bolted from the table, overjoyed at the unexpected reprieve.

Ruth, Ted, and Janeen all looked at Darla expectantly. Darla licked the last crumbs of cake from her fork and set it down, carefully lining it up with the edge of the place mat. "Excuse me for a moment, please," she murmured. "I have to go to the bathroom." She returned a few minutes later, her eyes bright, a small smile upon her lips. Happiness? Ruth thought uncertainly, or derision? You never know with her anymore. Ruth waited until Darla was seated across from her once more. The question would have to be asked, and now was as good a time as any, she thought.

"All right. What is it, Darla?" Ruth asked evenly. At Darla's continued silence, her mother added, "Your father and I have talked it over. We have agreed not to be angry, though you've probably ruined one of the best opportunities of your life. You are a smart girl, so obviously you know that already." Ruth cringed inwardly. She hadn't meant to be openly critical. "You wouldn't drop out and come home to talk to us unless this were important," Ruth continued, struggling to be more diplomatic. Ted stared blankly at the ruins of his chocolate cake.

Darla stood, pushing up the sleeves that hung from her slender arms. She helped herself to a large slice of cake and then sat again, still not speaking. She lifted a mouthful of cake and chewed it appreciatively. Finally she spoke.

"Great stuff, Mom. I've just been craving this cake. The whole dinner was great." Ruth forced a smile in thanks, feeling her jaw clench behind it. She would not give in to this callous manipulation, she vowed. She could wait as long as she had to. She drummed her plump fingers on the side of her glass.

As her parents and sister sat watching, Darla happily polished off her second helping of dessert. No answers were forthcoming.

Ruth bit back angry questions, keeping her thoughts to herself. All right, she just got here. She's tired, Ruth reasoned. In the past, she remembered, Darla had often seemed so tired as to be almost incoherent. She'd pushed herself beyond the limits of endurance in her studies and had to be nearly forced to rest. She had to get her stamina back. Ruth could wait a while. She rubbed at a tiny stain on the tablecloth with her napkin, at last sliding her plate over it.

Finally she spoke. "Let's talk tomorrow, Darla. Not about the cute guys at school or hairstyles or the book you just read. We'll really talk." Ruth shot Darla a look that she hoped was reassuring but stern. Darla nodded obediently. Ted sighed and said he guessed he'd better go over those papers in his briefcase. Janeen went to phone a friend. Darla continued to smile secretively. "Tomorrow," Ruth repeated firmly.

But that tomorrow had not come. All attempts at serious discussion had been rebuffed by Darla. And despite a few days' rest at home, she continued to look haggard.

Ruth tried to convince herself that all Darla needed was a few more days of rest. If she would only stop running every day, as Ruth had suggested, to let her body recover from traveling. Then she would feel better; then she would talk. Why did Darla insist on going against plain common sense and keep wearing herself out?

It was infuriating to Ruth to watch Darla's deliberate casualness as she turned her family inside out with worry. Ruth wondered which was worse, waiting for Darla to tell them what the problem was or dealing with the mysterious problem itself? Often Ruth's eyes would meet Ted's: calm, calm, they soothed.

But how could she remain calm, Ruth railed inwardly, when Darla's life could be falling apart? Darla had been sick—she claimed it was the flu. But what about those food cravings? Her excessive appetite? Her fatigue? Ted's calm gaze could not quiet Ruth's worst fear, that their eldest daughter was pregnant. No matter how often Ted urged Ruth to wait, to let Darla tell them in her own time, Darla was still secretive and irritable, and her mood swings were even wilder than they used to be.

As Darla's presence in the home waned to a lurking shadow, Ruth's waxed stronger. She paced and ranted and laundered and folded and scrubbed at her frustrations with almost inhuman vigor. All the while she wondered where Darla would go to have the baby, how to tell their relatives, how the boy's family would be told.

Ruth told herself as she shoveled the walks that she had failed as a mother. As she aligned the shoes at the back door by size, she admitted to herself that Darla was ungrateful. As she took down the front hall chandelier and washed it, cut glass teardrop by cut glass teardrop, she fumed that no one appreciated her efforts. The children kept busy, away from their mother, and Ruth's brow grew darker and more drawn every day. Still, her pale daughter refused to talk about it. The house sparkled.

Ruth was thankful that in those first few days, Darla had managed to avoid the painful verbal battles that had wounded herself and other family members in times past. Darla always stopped short of the explosions that had so often erupted over them all. Ruth thought this a sign of Darla's growing maturity and self-control.

Now Ruth reflected that she'd been mistaken. Darla was more out of control than ever. In the last couple of days, Ruth had seen the Darla she recognized from high school: brooding, petulant, angry. Darla's communication had become almost solely the shrewish, demanding, and relentless identification of family members' faults. She had reverted to damaging patterns: stealing Janeen's clothes, taking money from her mother's purse, raging at her father if he did not know the exact location of the car keys.

Ruth admitted to herself that life had been easier when Darla was at college in Utah.

It was easy to believe that she was all right, at school, away from the mother and sister she had so often blamed for her erratic behavior.

Easy to believe until this morning.

How had she said it? wondered Ruth. She tried to recall the way Darla had told her that morning. Ruth had left home to go to choir practice at nine. She'd reentered the house quietly an hour later, through the garage. Ted and the children had gone to visit Nana. Ruth did not expect to find anyone at home.

It was soon apparent by the sounds coming from the main floor bathroom that someone was there. Someone who was very ill. Perhaps Darla again. Late last night, when everyone else was asleep, Ruth had heard Darla lock herself in the bathroom, turn on the fan and the faucet, and throw up.

Ruth knocked tentatively at the pastel door. She forced her voice to be level. "Hello, Darla? Is that you? Are you all right, sweetheart?"

The sound of the faucet being turned nearly drowned Darla's voice. "Mom?" she called, her voice shaking. "Hi!"

"Darla!" Ruth's voice was strained. "Honey, are you okay? Can I help?"

The water stopped running. The door opened, and Darla, lithe and fair, stood on one slippered foot. Although she was usu-ally fastidious about her appearance, Darla's shirt was untucked, her strawberry-blonde hair in tangled waves about her shoulders. Her leather belt hung, undone, from her jeans.

"Oh, it's nothing. Just a touch of the flu, I guess. I feel much better now." Darla did not look at her mother as she spoke. She traced the pattern of flowers on the wallpaper inside the bath-room doorway. "You know, I like yellow roses a lot more than these blue ones. I wish these were yellow. It would be so much brighter in here with yellow . . ." her voice trailed off. Ruth fought back a retort about Darla's never being satisfied and stepped toward her, touching her on the shoulder. Her daughter smiled curtly, darted around her, and walked away.

"So," Darla's voice was brisk as she strode toward the kitchen. "You're home early." She flipped a cupboard door open easily and selected a glass. "I need a drink of water."

"You're positive you're okay now?" Ruth's suspicions grew. "I mean, last night . . ."

Darla looked up quickly. "Last night? I thought you were sleeping."

"You're shivering, Darla."

"Oh, it's so much colder here than Utah. I guess I'm just not used to it. I'm fine, really."

"I could take you to the Medi-Clinic. Are you sure?"

"Yup. Definitely. Well, maybe I'll stay home from church this afternoon. I'll see how it goes."

"Right. Well, if you need anything, let me know." Ruth's voice was even now. It did not betray her anger and hurt at being shut out once more. She would not give Darla the satisfaction. "You should probably lie down." She tried to appear unconcerned at Darla's lack of candor, yawning. "I think that's what I'm going to do."

She tugged at the belt of her dress. "I shouldn't have worn this to choir," she said. "I can hardly sit in it for more than fifteen minutes. How times have changed." She let out a relieved sigh as she removed the belt.

As she circled the belt around her dimpled hand, she watched Darla surreptitiously. Her daughter's glance was hard, shrewd. Then Darla nodded, smiling that sphinxlike smile, drained her glass, and placed it in the dishwasher. The girl was fluid in her grace, Ruth thought, like a dancer or a gymnast. A young woman who, as Ruth's friend Rhonda had remarked, "could wear flour sacks and look great."

A couple of years ago Darla had lost her puppy fat and grown chicly waiflike. How could she be that slim and still have a bust-line? Ruth wondered. She felt a twinge of envy as Darla unzipped her jeans and smoothed her shirt over flat, angular hips. She's not showing yet, Ruth thought. Can't be very far along.

Darla cinched her belt tightly and fluffed her hair back. She was awfully cool for someone who had just been violently ill, thought Ruth. She eyed her daughter critically, folding her arms across her chest, silently daring Darla to speak, to say it once and for all. Darla met her mother's glance; and then she turned delib-erately, walked to the family room, and clicked on the TV.

Say it! Ruth wanted to yell in exasperation, to kick against the wall that Darla had so skillfully erected between them. Ruth's whole being flooded with determination. I will find out right now, she told herself, and put an end to this charade. She strode purposefully toward the family room but then stopped, the inten-sity draining from her limbs.

Darla, eyes closed, was stretched out in a recliner, the unseen television squawking before her. Angular and thin, she looked like a dried flower threatened by the merest breath of air. The drapes were half-closed, and in the bluish light cast by the TV, Ruth saw dark hollows beneath her daughter's eyes, in her cheeks, at the base of her neck. The recliner cradled Darla, hardly bigger than a child in the large chair. Her thin arms hung limply from beneath a heavy knitted afghan, bony wrists and skeletal hands dangling white, almost glowing in the dimness. Her pale face, sur-rounded by wisps of hair, was eerily still.

Ruth turned, her heart aching with tenderness and fear. Not

now. It was not so important to shake the truth from her daughter right now. She fought down the dread welling up inside her.

Ruth left the family room and climbed the stairs slowly, her knees objecting with small cracking sounds. She ruminated as she rose, step by step, up the curving staircase. Darla wanted to stay home from church today. Why? Guilt? But she was always anxious to have time alone. To be here in the house by herself. It seemed she could hardly wait to get the family all out and away.

Ruth entered the master bedroom and paused before the open closet door, choosing a bright pink velour caftan. The color always gave her a lift. Gratefully Ruth stepped out of the red and white polka-dot dress and rolled down the constricting pantyhose. She felt her way into the caftan, arms above her head. As her face popped from the neckline, Ruth stopped moving, her arms still in the air.

Was Darla indeed pregnant? It would account for so much. Heaven knows, Ruth told herself, going to a Church university is no guarantee that a girl will be pure. There were always men who would take advantage . . . and Darla had been morally shaky at times, certainly . . . but could she really be . . . ? Many women vomited often during pregnancy. Ruth herself had. And Darla had been craving burritos, she said, and chocolate cake. And then, she was so tired . . . Ruth's mind again scuttled through the days since Darla's arrival, looking for clues. Everything she thought of seemed to echo her first conviction. Her young, nineteen-year-old daughter, brilliant with promise, was pregnant.

I'm jumping to conclusions, Ruth chided herself hopefully, almost desperately. She racked her brain, trying to remember any mention of men in Darla's frequent phone calls home. She had said she was dating, that she could go out with any one of a

number of young men. She called her male friends her Herd of
Nerds. That didn't sound to Ruth as if Darla were interested in
any of them, not in a romantic way. Yet Ruth's stomach grew
tight at the terrible possibility.

She was seized with a thought and hurried to the upstairs
bathroom, the one Darla used. She glanced into the cupboard
under the sink. No sanitary napkins. That didn't prove anything,
Ruth scolded herself. Even if there were, they could be Janeen's.
Ruth splashed cold water on her face. She imagined Ted's eyes:
calm, calm. She breathed deeply.

Ruth coughed. There was a sour smell in this room, though
she had cleaned it thoroughly only a day before. She sniffed and
then reopened the cupboard below the sink, peering farther into
its depths. A very smelly, wet rag was heaped at the back of the
cupboard. The painted wood around it had bubbled and blistered.
Grimacing, Ruth picked up the rag reluctantly, held it between
thumb and fingertip—a parody of a great lady with her lace
hanky—and dropped it with disgust down the laundry chute,
noticing spatters on the walls as she did so. Ruth washed her
hands carefully, her mind again on Darla and her possible . . .
No. She flicked drops of water from her hands into the sink,
found a towel, and then turned and shuffled tiredly back to her
room.

I'm probably overreacting again, she thought doubtfully.
Darla is just tired and stressed from school. She's had to keep her
marks up to keep her scholarship. She's sick, that's all. If she were
pregnant, I would know. A mother knows. The phrase was comforting. A mother knows, she repeated.

Now, as Ruth held the hymnbook in front of her and tried to
study the wavering dots there, she marveled at her blindness.

Later that morning she had learned painfully that a mother doesn't always know. A mother can be oblivious.

Ruth had remained seated on the bed, filing her nails distractedly as she pondered her daughter's behavior, when she'd heard Darla's footsteps on the stairs. There was the sound of Darla rummaging in her own room, and then the girl appeared in Ruth's doorway, a magazine in her hand.

Darla leaned on the door frame, one foot again tucked behind her, alternately smiling and biting her lip. She half-hid her mouth with a hand for a moment, her eyes circling about the room. The magazine was clutched across her chest, a perfect model shining from the glossy cover.

"Mom?" Darla asked, almost shyly. Her gaze was focused on the light fixture above her. Ruth looked at her daughter with concern, glimpsing her own anxious face in the mirror. Thoughts chased through her head: I will not open my mouth and say hurtful things. We will overcome this. She can go to Reba and Harold's until the baby is born . . . Ruth forced her brow to become smooth, her eyes to become compassionate. She willed herself to understand. This was her child, her firstborn.

"I kind of wanted to tell you something. I probably should have told you before this . . . " Darla's eyes met Ruth's and then skipped over to the headboard.

Ruth pushed the nail file into the soft flesh of her palm. I will be calm, she told herself. I will not grab her by the shoulders and demand to know the boy's name.

Darla shifted to her other foot. "You know I've been sick a lot." Ruth nodded impatiently. "Well, it isn't just the flu. It's . . . " Darla's eyes searched her mother's face. She reached out a hand and then withdrew it. "It's more serious than that," she said at last. A deep sigh escaped Ruth. She felt very heavy, as if her body were being pulled down into the comfort of her bed, to sleep and forget.

"Mom . . . I'm bulimic."

"What?" Ruth's astonished smile was real. Inwardly she rejoiced. She's not pregnant! Not pregnant! It's going to be all right!

In Ruth's sudden relief, she hadn't understood her daughter's confession. "What, honey? What did you say?" Ruth wanted to laugh out loud at her own foolishness. Of course Darla wasn't pregnant. "Tell me again, sweetheart. I didn't quite catch that." Not pregnant, not pregnant, not pregnant. Ruth pushed her relief aside and tried to snatch the thread of intimacy dangled tantalizingly by her daughter.

"Bulimic. I have bulimia. An eating disorder. I eat; I throw up. I have done it for two years, and it's getting worse." Darla paused and then added firmly, "I could die." Ruth looked up quickly. Darla wore the enigmatic half-smile that was disturbingly familiar to Ruth. Her eyes were upon her mother's face, searching for a reaction.

"Die? Oh, surely not." Ruth waved the nail file dismissively in her daughter's direction. She remembered Darla as a child, streaking toward the traffic, pulling herself up short at the curb. She would turn and laugh as Ruth, terrified, ran shouting toward her, outstretched hands shaking, and Janeen huddled in fear behind. She wants me to be upset, Ruth thought. I won't give her the satisfaction. Darla had always been overly dramatic in her tales of woe, searching for buttons to push. Not this time, you don't, Ruth vowed.

"I'm sure this is something we can handle, Darla," she said aloud. "An eating disorder? It doesn't sound all that bad." Ruth patted the bed beside her, trying not to let her relief show. Just a teenage girl diet thing, after all, she thought. Nothing that would ruin her daughter's life. Ruth sighed gently. She'd been a decent mother after all, she assured herself. "Come and sit down, Darla. We'll talk." Ruth mentally added, And wipe that smirk off your face.

Darla walked toward the bed but did not sit. "Here. There's an article in this magazine." She stood uncomfortably for a moment. "You can ask me about it later if you want." The magazine whirled and landed on the bed with a quiet thud. Darla fled from the room. Her waves of red-gold hair bobbed as she turned to glimpse her mother's startled face on the way out. A moment later, Darla's bedroom door slammed.

"*Eating Disorders—Starving for Attention,*" proclaimed the magazine cover. It seemed to Ruth that Darla could hardly be starving—she'd eaten steadily since she got home. As she flipped to the touted article, she was prepared to put this whole episode down as just another one of Darla's bids for attention. Some children were like that. Just Darla being Darla. But what Ruth read, there between photos of fantastically thin and ethereally beautiful women, changed her mind.

The article started by quoting a woman who led group therapy sessions for bulimics:

"*Bulimics are truly killing themselves to achieve someone else's ideal of perfect womanhood.*"

Killing themselves? Probably just journalistic hyperbole, Ruth thought. But her doubt became concern as she read farther.

"*Bulimics purge themselves, in part, to attain their idea of a perfect body. Often they are perfectionists and have to be the best at everything.*"

That's Darla. Ruth thought uneasily of the trophy cabinet.

"*About four percent of the young-adult female population of*

North America is estimated to be full-blown bulimics—that is, they
binge-eat and then induce vomiting to avoid gaining weight. As many
as 15 to 30 percent of North America's young women may have occasional bulimic episodes."

How many of Darla's friends? Ruth wondered. How many of
my friends' daughters?

"These girls are dying to be thin. They associate fat with being
bad, unlovable. And the media's portrayal of so-called 'perfect 10s'
does nothing to dispel their idea that the thinner the better."

Nothing new there, Ruth thought. It was ever thus. She
knew only too well the self-loathing, the price one paid for being
fat in a thin world.

"Fifteen percent of bulimics will die as a result of uncontrolled
bingeing and purging."

Die! What is Darla fooling around with? This is no teenage
weight-loss fad. Bingeing and purging? Ruth's stomach knotted.
Darla couldn't really be like that, she told herself. She couldn't be
in any danger. The flesh on Ruth's arms crawled. As she read, she
inwardly compared her daughter to the characteristics listed:

"Bulimics binge-eat, occasionally consuming as much as 50,000
calories a day. Then they induce vomiting and start the cycle again."

So much food disappears from this house when Darla is
home. And she's always baking more.

"The stomach acid of a bulimic will eat away at her tooth enamel,
causing permanent damage. Her electrolytes will plummet dangerously,
causing disorientation and fatigue."

All those times when I thought she'd been studying too hard,
when she was so wiped out . . .

"As she receives no calcium from the food she eats, her bones will
become porous and break easily. She will suffer from osteoporosis."

She is becoming a brittle old lady at nineteen. Her body is consuming itself.

The next paragraph confirmed it:

"The esophagus and other tissues of a bulimic will be slowly eaten away by stomach acids."

Darla hardly sings any more. She says her throat hurts.

"Bulimics abuse laxatives in an effort to 'cleanse' their body of all food."

Ruth groaned. Darla's belt had been loose, her shirt untucked.

"Her menstrual periods will eventually stop, as her body is experiencing a famine."

Ruth felt sick as she recalled those jutting hipbones that had caused her a twinge of envy less than an hour before.

Darla was drawn, tired, irritable, controlling, often cold; she exercised strenuously . . . Ruth read the list of symptoms with a growing, fearful certainty. There was a dismally low cure rate for eating disorders. These women starved their bodies of nutrients— starved themselves to death, knowing they were doing so but unable to quit. Bulimia was that addictive.

One doctor quoted said it was *"worse than drugs. They could try that once and quit. But for these girls, it's once and they're hooked. It has been labeled an obsession, an addiction, an emotional illness. One thing's for sure. Unless they get medical attention and psychotherapy, it's just a matter of time before they do themselves permanent damage, even die."*

For a split second Ruth wondered if pregnancy would have been better news, after all.

Ruth continued to read. *"These young women often come from homes where the mother is dominating . . . and the father absent or distant.*" Ruth snorted. Not in this case, surely? Why do the parents always get blamed?

Ruth let herself fall backwards upon the bed, the pink velour falling about her rounded body in gentle folds. *Is* it my fault? Did I try to make her perfect? Is it my fault?

Fifteen percent die, she had read. Darla could be one of those, if all this was true. Darla had said she'd been doing it for two years. How come I never noticed it? How did she hide it from me?

Ruth hardly dared ask herself the next question. What kind of a mother wouldn't see her child's distress? What kind of a mother am I? She grabbed fistfuls of the quilted bedspread. What could we have done to make her this way? she whispered to the ceiling.

Ruth's chest ached. She rolled on to her side, pushed by the enormity of the implications. Curling her body inward, she covered her head with her arms. She didn't want to know. Tears, hot and silent, slid from Ruth's blue eyes. Behind her closed eyelids she saw Darla at twelve, her hips starting to curve, Janeen a twig in comparison. "Better cut down on the bread, Darla," Ruth heard herself say. And at fifteen—Darla was athletic, rounded and firm, Janeen a willow. The boys were already following Janeen with their eyes, a fact that did not escape her older sister. Did I approve of Janeen's body more? Did I shame Darla? Ruth could not remember doing so. But what, she asked herself, what did I teach without words?

From downstairs rose the sound of kitchen cupboards—open-shut, open-shut, and then the refrigerator door. The noises stopped. Darla must have found something there to try and fill the unfillable hole within her. The scrupulously clean house was ominously quiet, empty as Darla's insatiable void.

Ruth lay worrying, half-listening to the low noises from the radio, still staring at the ceiling as if expecting it to offer answers. Darla's footsteps at last ascended the stairs. She went into her bedroom.

Ruth waited, hearing cars drive by, the shouts of neighbors, dogs barking. Once in a while her chest heaved in a shudder, and her beringed hand pushed a tear away and fell to her side once more.

Darla's bedroom door clicked open. Ruth snapped to a sitting position. Darla was running down the hall. With a speed that amazed herself, Ruth half-rolled, half-jumped from the bed and ran to the upstairs hallway, folds of cloth rippling and flowing around her legs.

She stopped, a pink velour mountain, in front of the bathroom door, her bosom heaving. "No," Ruth said firmly, breathlessly, her small chin jutting. "This has to stop." She crossed her arms over her chest.

"Mom! Move! Get out of my way!"

"No," Ruth repeated. "You are killing yourself."

Darla's eyes were wild. "You don't understand, Mom. I have to go in there. I have to!"

"No." Ruth was obdurate.

Darla's face became a grotesque mask, twisted and reddened in fury. "Leave me alone, you cow!" Ruth flinched. Darla's voice was acid. "As if you're so perfect. Two hundred pounds of perfect! Just move! Move!" Her voice rose to a scream. She shook her fists in the air with a growl of frustration and then turned to run downstairs. Ruth caught her daughter short.

"No."

Ruth gazed angrily and then compassionately at the frail girl who crumpled, sobbing, at her feet. Darla wept, ranted, cursed as she railed against Ruth. But Darla was weakened, and her mother, for all her soft appearance, was a strong woman. She knelt, holding Darla's shoulders. "Honey, you've got to try."

Darla wrenched away from her mother and ran down the stairs, a greyhound on the scent. Her hair flew as she took the stairs three at a time. She grabbed the newel post with both hands and swung herself around the corner, as if her very life depended on her speed.

Ruth did not follow. She sat slumped against the banister. She listened to Darla flee to her echoing prison, click the door lock, flip on the whirring fan, turn the faucet to full rush—the several steps repeated without thought by one who has done them over and over—Ruth listened to these things. And then she listened to her eldest daughter throw up. Again.

Spatters on the wallpaper. The sour smell. The awful, stinking rag that had festered in the dark cupboard. I should have known, Ruth told herself. How could I not have known? She huddled against the banister, her red-gold curls flattened against the hard planes of the unyielding wooden rails, her wide feet planted on the step before her. Her massive shoulders shook under the soft pink fabric as she began to cry.

Ted and the kids arrived half an hour later, finding Ruth subdued and Darla prowling the house like a sated panther. Ted knew upon seeing Ruth's face that they had to talk. At first he didn't believe it.

"She's just doing this to make a scene, honey. You know how she is," he said gently, sitting beside his wife on the bed. Ruth shook her head and handed him the magazine.

"No, it's true. I mean, maybe she is doing it for attention, but she's definitely doing it. She's done it twice this morning already." Ruth choked back a sob. "And I've been thinking about it, Ted.

Remember the missing Halloween candy? The leftovers that disappeared almost as soon as they were put in the fridge? Well, read this. You'll see. She has all the symptoms."

Ruth sat, head in hands, as Ted read the article through. "I still find this hard to believe, Ruth. How could anyone make themselves throw up? It's so . . . " His voice trailed off. "I mean, I keep thinking of this little girl in a pink dress with all these ringlets and shiny shoes with ruffled socks. And then I think of her . . . "

"She's not your cute baby girl, Ted. She's nineteen. She's messed up. She needs help." As if at an unseen signal, Ted and Ruth lowered themselves from the bed and knelt at its edge. They prayed for the little girl in ruffled socks, the stick-thin teenager down the hall, for the spirit that was their daughter, Darla. The girl she could be, the girl she was—somewhere inside, without illness or anger or shame.

"Amen." Ted and Ruth knelt in silence for several minutes.

"There must be someone we could ask."

"How about Rod Drake? He's a psychologist. He must know someone."

"Wasn't there a girl in the Twelfth Ward who was anorexic or something? What was her name? We could call her parents."

For the first time since Ruth had talked in the kitchen with Darla this morning, she felt the weight of hopelessness lift slightly. "Faith," she admonished them both. "We have to have faith." Ted's eyes held hers, reassuring and calm.

Then there was the Sunday rush. Putting on good clothes, uncomfortable shoes and belts, getting their appearance just right. Of course, the kitchen was off-limits. It was Fast Sunday. But Ruth's practiced ear detected Darla rummaging frantically in her dresser drawers and closet. For what? Ruth wondered. She was careful not to let Darla near a bathroom again until they had left the house.

And that, at least, had worked. Ruth looked down toward the aisle. Janeen was sitting at the end of the pew, Darla beside her, and then Ted and herself. On the other side of Ruth sat Kevin and Megan. The whole family was here, all safe, and Darla was not throwing up. Ruth straightened her shoulders and sat up taller as the bishop finished speaking.

The first notes of the sacrament hymn sounded. A movement to Ruth's left caught her eye. She turned her head in time to see Darla push past her sister's knees and dart down the aisle of the chapel, faces turned toward her in curiosity. Helplessness rose within Ruth. "Not again!" she whispered. Ruth, long used to taking charge and managing, must sit and watch her daughter destroy herself. Watch her bring a sore curse upon the heads of her family with her twisted affliction.

Janeen glanced toward her mother and then rose quickly and ran after Darla. Darla, her older, brighter, thinner sister. Ruth shifted awkwardly in the pew, almost hovering there, uncertain whether to follow. Janeen circled an arm about Darla's bony shoulders as the two girls reached the door at the back of the chapel.

Ruth slumped back into the pew, fighting tears. Ted squeezed her hand. She turned to face him. Calm, his look reminded her. Calm. She rested her head on his shoulder for a moment. "We will get help," Ruth whispered to her husband, quietly. "She will not face this alone. She will not be one of that fifteen percent. I know it. I just know it." She squeezed his hand.

JANEEN: REAL SUGAR

Janeen Boynton stretched her long legs out in front of her, wishing her kneecaps did not make such angular knobs under her ribbed leggings. Her birthday was coming up. She wondered if Mom would let her have a party. Probably not, the way things were at home right now. But eighteen was special. Maybe she would go out to Moxie's with some of her girlfriends.

Eighteen. Janeen sighed. Major birthday. Relief Society time. She had wondered about Relief Society a lot lately. What did they do in there? Was it like Laurels, only with a read-along manual? For sure they won't be talking about guys in Relief Society!

Janeen pictured herself with her mother and her mother's friends, debating the finer points of sanctification. Then at a table at homemaking, whipping up a padded picture frame. Yuck. Maybe she could ask Sister Sullivan, the Primary president, about a calling in the Primary instead.

Janeen had often seen the large seal of the Relief Society, golden and framed. "Charity Never Faileth," it intoned, as it hung on the wall of the Relief Society room alongside cross-stitched pictures of women who inexplicably wore long dresses, praying or playing with husbands and children in modern clothing. Janeen twirled a lock of long brown hair. You'd never catch me in a dress like that. Not in a million years. How would you run for a bus or ride a bike or even go up and down stairs without breaking your neck?

"Charity Never Faileth." Charity, compassion, understanding. All adult words. Janeen wondered if they would fit 'as awkwardly on her as one of those encumbering dresses. It seemed that Janeen's world was rapidly changing from a Clearasil to an Oil of Olay state, and she didn't know if she was ready. It would be so good to finally be out of high school, she thought, to be at last an adult, in control of her own life. She could go on to college and be on her own: study when she wanted, come and go as she pleased without her mother's curfews or rules.

So many decisions now. Big ones, that'll affect the rest of my life. And I can't help feeling that so much is expected of me once I start Relief Society and I'm in there with The Sisters—although Darla was in Relief Society at BYU, and it hasn't changed her much. She's still as crabby as ever, Janeen thought.

Janeen's stomach growled. She sighed and rolled her eyes. "Church has barely started, and I'm starving already," she leaned over and whispered to her sister Darla.

"No kidding," was Darla's bored reply. "Got any gum? I was gonna get some, but Dad wouldn't let us stop at the 7-Eleven because it's Sunday. Honestly! It's not like I was going to get groceries or something. Everyone knows that fasting gives you bad breath. Thanks," Darla added as Janeen dug to the bottom of a battered leather purse and came up with a piece of gum. Darla quickly unwrapped it and began to chew. Her expression went sour. "What is this? Sugarless bubble gum? Yuck." Her voice had risen above a whisper, and the girls' father turned to silence them.

Janeen rolled her eyes once toward Darla, who ignored her.

Darla ignored everybody these days. Janeen turned her head, glancing around her to see where the good-looking Patrick Klassen was seated. Her eyes rested on two little girls, Janie and Megan Rasmussen, sitting like bookends on either side of their mother. They reached across their mother to touch each other, whispering messages, their pale blonde heads almost touching.

Once, she and Darla had been like that, Janeen remembered. Darla had been closer to her than anyone else on earth. They had played together all day long in years past, during summer holidays that seemed to stretch elastically for months. They had taken bicycle picnics to Fish Creek Park nearly every day of the summer when they were home. And when they were at the lake, they had their own world in a clearing among the poplars. Sand castles, sunburns, pesky cousins, the smell of Coppertone—a wave of memory washed into Janeen's mind, as fresh and clear as a wave from Echo Lake itself.

One summer afternoon they had happily played for hours beneath the canopy of the poplars. Janeen had been about seven, she reckoned, so Darla would have been eight and a half. A cinder block had stood in a small clearing; this was the chair. An old apron of their mother's was the hairdressing cape. They had a big comb. They were going to play Hair Salon. Both girls washed their hair in shivery water from a bucket, gasping and squealing as it splashed on their sun-hot skin and trickled down the backs of their matching bathing suits. They laughed as they wrapped towels around their heads, making lopsided turbans.

"We look like Mom and Sister Fitzpatrick now," Darla clapped her hands. "When she comes over for Mom to do her hair." She paused conspiratorially. "Look what I've got!" With a flourish Darla produced the small pair of sewing scissors she had found in the cutlery drawer. "This is going to be so fun! You first, Neener," she said. "Sit down!"

Janeen hesitated, her heart thumping. A rivulet of cold water snaked down her back. "Uh-uh, Gar. I want my hair long. I want to be a mermaid." She dug a toe in the dirt in front of her. An ant scurried across it.

"Well, you can't be," was Darla's complacent answer. "You don't have a fin. And after yours is done, you can cut mine. Now sit down."

Janeen reluctantly sat. The rough cinder block was an uncomfortable seat, narrow and teetering. "Gar" set about busily combing her sister's hair.

"Did I tell you about my new dress?" Gar asked in a singsong voice. "I got it for the symphony next week. It's perfectly lovely. Pink and purple, with a big long skirt and a bow on the back. Divine." Snip. Snip.

Gar was right, this was fun, Neener told herself, although her heart pounded in her throat. After a few moments she said, in an extra polite, grown-up voice, "Why don't you borrow my parasol to take? It has flowers on it, and a ruffle around the edge. It is pink and green and purple." From the corner of her eye, Neener caught Gar's intent face. Gar was biting her lip and looking out of one eye as the scissors neared Neener's ear. Snip. Neener jumped slightly. Her hand flew up to check her ear. Gar moved around to the back of Neener's head. Snip. Snip. Clumps of damp, dark hair fell on the ground about the cinder block. Bits of it tickled under Neener's bathing suit. She wriggled on the scratchy cinder block.

"I'm almost done. Sit still." Neener obediently sat still until Gar was finally done. Her sister stood back to look critically at her work. She smiled brightly at Neener. "You look just beautiful. Better than a mermaid." But Gar sounded a bit uncertain.

Neener stood up and untied the apron from her neck, letting the prickly pieces of hair fall from its folds. "Your turn," she said, turning to Gar. She held out her hand for the scissors.

Gar took a step backwards. "No." She threw the scissors. They stuck into the ground between them, teetering on one blade like a ballerina.

"You promised," Neener reminded her. Her voice was firm.

"But I don't want a haircut!" Gar's freckled face reddened.

Neener set her jaw. "You promised."

"No. I won't."

Neener walked over to the scissors and yanked them from the ground. It was strange not to have her hair fall around her shoulders when she bent over. She stood and reached a hand toward Gar. "You promised," she said matter-of-factly.

Neener put her hand on Gar's head and took a fistful of damp, coppery hair. It felt like wet shoelaces. She held it close to the scalp and opened the scissors as far as she could. Gar's eyes were wide. Snip. It was shorter than Neener had expected.

Gar's eyes grew even wider at the lifeless snake of hair that hung from her sister's hand.

"It looks beautiful," Neener said, doubtfully, appraising Gar's head. "We might as well finish it now, or it will look funny." Gar opened her mouth, her face red again. "It was your big idea," Neener reminded her.

Gar shut her mouth and sat down. She soon forgot her reluctance and was again borne on the spirit of adventure. The two girls resumed their ever-so-adult discussion of clothes, expanding the conversation to include restaurants and tantrum-throwing children, laughing over them in the weary and wise way of mothers.

"Oh, now! You know we wouldn't trade them for anything!"
Neener said in a knowing voice, echoing a snippet of overheard
baby shower conversation. "Everyone has their little faults." Gar
nodded sagely and then stopped as a coil of hair fell into her lap.

When they were finished, dark and red-gold hair lay entan-
gled in the sunlight at their feet. The summer air felt delicious
on their backs and necks. Both girls held their hands up, feeling
their heads, and giggling.

And then, Janeen recalled, Mom found us. Ruth Boynton
walked into the clearing, pregnant and hot, and saw the bicol-
ored coils of hair, her daughters' mowed heads, and their sun-
burnt, smiling faces. She screamed. The girls stared at each other
in shock. And Ruth's scream had risen high over the trees, curling and dipping, and unexpectedly turned into a laugh. A long,
high, gasping, hysterical laugh. Ruth fell to her knees in the dirt,
her hands on her round belly, face streaming. Her whole body
shook, the lump that would be Megan rising and falling. Ruth
stretched out her arms and pulled the girls towards her.

"Oh! Oh! It's awful!" She laughed harder, hugging the girls to
her, their damp shaggy heads against her yellow cotton maternity
smock. "What will I do with you two?" Gar and Neener peered at
one another across their mother's heaving breasts and giggled,
their skinny arms around Ruth's huge belly, each finding the
other's hand and squeezing.

We were best friends once, Janeen thought ruefully, as she
shifted on the pew and glanced at her sister's profile. Darla sat
masticating gum as if it were the closest thing to food that she'd
seen in weeks. When had that friendship changed? Janeen wondered. When we got interested in boys, maybe. Started hanging
out with different kids, dating different kinds of guys. And we've
never been close since.

Janeen winced at the memories of Darla's angry face swearing at her, using words that Janeen had never heard anyone in their family use, finding any way she could to hurt her little sister. Suddenly everything had become a competition. Darla had to have more dates, better clothes, more fun than anyone on an out-ing. Although Janeen was a better than average student, Darla's grades had always surpassed her sister's. Darla waved report cards in Janeen's face and teased her about being stupid. She continued to run track, growing lean and wolfish, chiding Janeen for her lack of activity. Darla became vigilant at ensuring her own suc-cesses, and it seemed as if any success of Janeen's was a failure on Darla's part. To Darla's chagrin, Janeen was the one surrounded by friends, the one kidnapped by a group of girls on her birthday and taken to a movie, or given a surprise party. Darla had become increasingly sullen and rude to Janeen's friends. Often she hung up on them when they phoned.

Janeen had been hoping that it would be different when her sister came home from BYU. Maybe the fact that she was hav-ing trouble with her grades, or whatever the problem was, would make Darla more human. She turned to look at the Rasmussen girls and then at Darla once more. It just wasn't happening. Whatever was bugging Darla, she wasn't talking.

Janeen gazed around the chapel. Everyone looked so intent and serious. The light was slightly yellowish, and it was getting very warm. She felt claustrophobic. It must be like this for the lizards in her brother Kevin's terrarium, she thought. She leaned back and lifted the heavy dark hair off the back of her neck and then turned her head to study her older sister. Darla looked as if she were perched on the cinder block seat, Janeen thought. Darla's eyes darted around the chapel, and her hands trembled slightly. Janeen wondered if it was just the light, or if Darla was paler than she used to be.

Janeen leaned over, letting her dark hair spill onto Darla's shoulder. Her voice held the friendly teasing lilt she had often used with her sister when they were children. "You look about as healthy as Lily Munster, Darla. What have you been doing to yourself at school?"

Darla said nothing but aimed a glance at her sister that was intended to wound. Janeen blinked. Same old Darla, she thought. "Take it easy! I'm sorry, I was just kidding." Janeen felt suddenly lonely. She hesitated and then touched her sister's hand. "Darla, are you all right?"

Darla's silence was very clearly intended to shut her sister up. She turned away, cracking her gum with a noise like a cap gun. At her father's glare, she stopped chewing and clenched her teeth. Still she would not turn toward her sister. Janeen could see the muscles in Darla's face working.

Without warning, Darla stood up and pushed past Janeen's bony knees, oblivious to the startled faces turned toward her. Darla's gait was jerky and quick as she hurried down the aisle toward the chapel doors, her dress a flag snapping in the wind.

Great. What's bugging her now? Janeen muttered to herself. She glanced at her mother, who looked scared. In a moment of sudden revelation, Janeen knew that things with Darla were worse than she'd thought. Darla's surly silences, her secretive behavior, and her waspish comments were more than just Darla being Darla. Things were much worse, Janeen realized, as she took in her mother's stricken expression.

Filled with resolve, Janeen rose and followed her sister down the aisle. She caught up with her as she was about to leave the chapel and put her arm around Darla's shoulder, first awkwardly and then with authority.

They did not speak as they entered the foyer. There were too many people there. Janeen propelled her reluctant sister into a darkened cloakroom, Darla's feet hissing across the carpet in protest.

The conversation consisted of sibilant whispers:

"What do you think you're doing?" Darla fumed.

"Me? I could ask you the same thing."

"I don't know what you're talking about."

"Fine, let me give you a hint." Janeen's voice was low and angry. "How about this: you come home from school with some deep dark secret, you look like you're seriously dying or something, you walk out of church before we even have the sacrament, and Mom looks at you as if you're about to self-destruct." Janeen stopped, her chest heaving, still holding Darla's thin arm in her grasp.

Darla opened and closed her mouth. She dropped her head, covering her face with her hands for several long seconds. Finally she took them away and tried to speak. The words did not come.

In a heartbeat, Janeen saw clearly that charity did not always wear long skirts and carry homemade rolls. Janeen considered her choices. She could drop Darla's scarecrow arm and go back into the chapel. She didn't have to be a capital-S Sister yet. Or she could try to help and probably feel the sting of Darla's venom as she did so.

Darla bit her lip and looked up at the ceiling and then at Janeen. The words seemed to be wrung out of her, falling like pieces of shriveled leaves in the dry air.

"I—I can't really talk about it." Tears sprang to Darla's blue eyes. Her face screwed itself into a tight knot, like a hurt child before she draws breath and begins to scream. Janeen made up her mind.

"Let's go somewhere and talk." With her free hand, she grabbed their jackets from their hooks. "Come on! I drove this morning—I've got the keys," Janeen urged her sister.

Darla shook her head wordlessly, sniffling.

"We have to, Darla," Janeen said grimly. She shoved her sister's arms into the ski jacket, as if Darla were a backward child, and shrugged on her own jacket. Janeen then pulled her relenting sister past the curious onlookers in the foyer and opened the glass doors to a chilling blast. She shepherded Darla across the parking lot toward the Boyntons' old brown van.

Janeen drove in silence, going just a little too fast on the icy road, straight to Fish Creek Park. Naked trees sped by. "I sure hope Mom doesn't go nuclear about this," Janeen murmured under her breath. Darla leaned against the door and held her face in her hands again.

Janeen was not very good at driving a standard yet. Darla's head bounced against the passenger-side window as her sister downshifted awkwardly over the gravel road and parked beneath the shelter of the big pines. Janeen shut off the engine, listening to Darla's quiet sobs. The snow-covered park was overcast with a lifeless pall, the sun lost behind a heavy quilt of gray. The trees stood mute and still, drooping slightly under their snowy burden, blocking the view from the main road. This was once their picnic spot, unvisited by either girl for years.

She had felt very grown up and in control as she steered the ponderous van. Now, as Janeen saw Darla's hands, white-knuckled and glistening with tears, she felt helpless. She fervently hoped it was true that "Charity Never Faileth." Heavenly Father, what do I say? Janeen begged silently. How can I help her? She had certainly seen Darla cry before, but always when she'd been enraged or physically hurt. These tears seemed to spring from somewhere in Darla that Janeen had never seen before. Vulnerable, lost, scared . . . not the confident, perfect, often obnoxious girl that Janeen had known as her big sister. This whole thing was strange to Janeen, and frightening. Who could have caused it? And was Janeen capable of helping her? Did those cross-stitched women sit in covered wagons in the valleys of the Wasatch and cry with each other?

She sat for a minute, deciding what to do. I have to know what it is, Janeen reasoned inwardly. She spoke at last. "Darla, what? What is it?"

Darla's torment escalated. She screamed, a wild tearing scream of suffering and rage. Her head was thrown back. Her eyes were scrunched up, her fists shaking in the air beside her head as her pain echoed from the metal walls of the old van.

And then she slumped against the door, exhausted by the strength of her feelings. Tears coursed down her face and fell unheeded into her lap. Janeen pulled a tissue from a crumpled box on the dashboard and handed it to her sister. She took Darla's arm gently. "Okay, Darla. What is going on?" Janeen said, her voice low and even.

Darla wadded her gum and shoved it into the tissue, twisting and wringing it until it was a lumpy mass. She hurled it angrily at the windshield. For a while she said nothing, the muscles of her face tight. Finally she spoke.

"Okay," she smiled bitterly, still facing the windshield. "I wasn't going to tell you. But you should know." She looked sideways at Janeen, through narrowed eyes as though to gauge the effect of her words. Then she continued, "Because maybe I wouldn't have this problem if it weren't for you."

Janeen's grip on Darla's arm tightened slightly. She told herself that she would not get pulled into it this time. Darla couldn't play that game any more. She let go of her sister's arm and asked coldly, "What?"

"I'm bulimic," Darla said slowly. Almost proudly, Janeen thought, her mind trying to grasp the implications of Darla's statement.

Janeen's blank expression seemed to irritate her sister. "You know," Darla continued. "It's an eating disorder, like anorexia. Except I eat. A lot. And then I throw it up."

Janeen pulled back into her seat, hugging herself. Her heart pounded. Her fault! She was stunned. How could it be her fault? Baffled anger rose within her, momentarily pushing aside compassion or any impulse for charity.

"My fault! Right! It's always my fault, or Mom's fault, or someone else's . . . " She squeezed her eyes closed and put her hands over her ears, trying to shut out Darla's crying. The long-skirted ladies had never had a sister like Darla. "Darla, you need *serious* help," Janeen said loudly, her hands still over her ears.

Darla suddenly pounded the brown plastic console between them. Startled, Janeen dropped her hands and watched, open-mouthed. "Why do you have to be so nice?" Darla demanded, punching the console as she barked the word *nice*. Copper-blonde hair hung in twisting ropes in front of her puffy eyes. Her face was a deep red. "So perfect." *Whack*. "And good." *Whack*. "And nice!" *Whack*.

Janeen struggled to push down her own anger and hurt. A fight would not solve this problem, she told herself; it never had in the past. And this was unlike the arguments over borrowed sweaters or ruined shoes. This was shaping up to be something monstrous. Her mind raced again in prayer. Please, Heavenly Father, help me know what to do!

Darla swung her head around to face Janeen. "Yes, it is your fault. Look at you!" She grabbed Janeen's wrist and held it up, her fingers digging in. "Look! Bones. Not a bit of fat. Anywhere. You and your perfect little body." Darla's voice became a mimicking singsong as she chanted, "Your perfect little body, and your perfect little face, and your perfect little personality! How am I supposed to compete with that?"

"You're sick, Darla." Janeen's voice was gentle.

"No. I was. I was sick of being the fat and ugly older sister. I was sick of having boys look at you and not me. I was sick of staying home while Little Miss Perfect went out to dinner and a movie with Rod Carpenter or Jamie Thurman or Gary Francis." Darla's eyes gleamed. She giggled mirthlessly. "I'm not sick now, Little Sister. Nope. Got loads of dates. Herds of nerds, gaggles of guys." She kept giggling. "Just because I have to puke to do it, am I sick?" Janeen saw tears in her sister's eyes. "Because I have to eat laxatives and stick a toothbrush down my throat so I can look like Cindy Crawford or Julia Roberts, or *you*, am I sick?" Her giggles turned to sobs and then to a thin, high wail. Darla's head lolled against the window. She opened her eyes and stared listlessly at the dark evergreens outside. Her arms hung loosely at her sides.

"Darla, are you serious? You really do that stuff? That's . . . "

"Gross? Disgusting? Twisted? Sick? Tell me one I haven't thought of." She folded her arms across her chest.

"No way! No way!"

"Janeen, I know every rest room on campus. I know what time of day they're the least busy. I know which ones have fans to drown out the noise. I know the fastest route from any given spot on campus to a bathroom." Her face was slack now, resigned and thin, the gray light shading the deep hollows of her cheeks. "I used to race from dorm to dorm in Helaman Halls looking for a free toilet."

Janeen did not reply. Darla sighed. "You want to know the best place to throw up? The Sky Room, at the Wilkinson Center. After about two o'clock, the professors and big shots have all eaten lunch and left. Noisy fan, hardly anyone around, nice setting." Darla snorted, "A bulimic's dream."

"But why? Why would you want to look like . . . this?" Janeen waved a hand toward Darla's wasted body. "I mean, you were always so strong, so confident. You know, athletic and . . . "

"Butch. Tough. Ugly."

"No! No way!"

Darla began to cry again. Blotches appeared on her pale skin. She closed her swollen eyelids. "Every time I looked in the mirror. Every time Mom didn't give me dessert. Or we went to the mall, and some guy would smile at you . . ." Her shoulders shook. As Darla bowed her head, her hair streaming over her face and shoulders, Janeen could count the individual vertebrae of her sister's neck.

Janeen slid over and sat on the console. She laid her hand on Darla's back, feeling the hard little hills of her spine beneath the jacket. She could not take her eyes from her sister's neck. "Darla," she whispered. "I never knew. I swear I never even thought of it—honest! I'm so sorry you felt like that." Janeen groaned. "Oh, Darla . . . " she pleaded earnestly. "Every time you ran the hundred-yard dash. Every time we played volleyball in Young Women. Every time we went waterskiing with Jason and Sandi. Every time I was killing myself to keep up to you on your bike. Perfect! You're the one who was always perfect. I envied the way you walked, just striding along like you owned the world, swinging your arms. I always wished I could have been more, well, more like you." Janeen's voice was quiet, her eyes filled with tears. "Darla, this is crazy. I can't believe you'd be jealous of *me*, with my nonexistent calf muscles and skinny arms. I always wanted to be *you*. And now look at you. What are you *doing* to yourself?"

Darla sighed. "You're right, you know." Darla's voice was quiet behind the curtain of hair. "It's not just you, Janeen, or Mom. It's not anyone. But it's everyone, everything." She turned toward Darla. "The gorgeous women, the models and actresses and singers—they're not jocks, Janeen. They're thin-thin-thin." She put her thumb and forefinger close together and peered at her sister through the opening. "Like this. Not linebackers." She blew out her bottom lip, ruffling her bangs. "Not like me, the way I was. I wasn't good enough, Janeen! For the first time in my life, I wasn't good enough." Her voice was bitter.

"When did it start?"

"A little over two years ago. Remember when Kenny Bates broke up with me?" Janeen nodded, and Darla continued. "He told his friends that I had a big rear end. That was the last straw."

"But Darla! Kenny Bates was such a dweeb! You were going to break up with him anyhow. Why would you care what he thought?" Janeen was perplexed.

"You don't get it. *He* broke up with *me*. That was the first time that's ever happened. I was always the one to break up, not the guy. This time, he did, because he thought I was ugly."

Janeen could hardly believe what she was hearing. "That was just some bogus excuse, Darla! Besides, even if someone is kind of—big—that doesn't mean they're *ugly*."

"You bet it does," Darla spat. Janeen shook her head. "So I

started purging then, making myself throw up—thinking it was only temporary. Then I realized that I could eat as much as I wanted and *never gain weight*. It was like, such freedom!" She shook her head, a wry smile on her lips.

"And now it isn't."

"No." Her voice was strangled. "Oh, Janeen, I'm so ashamed. Whenever I try to deal with this, when I think about things I've done—I feel such shame and guilt, and I just don't know how to stop it. I don't know if I can."

"And that's why you're home."

Darla nodded. "It was just—so out of control. My roommates found out about it. They had this meeting without me. They told me if I didn't call Mom and Dad, they would."

"Are you glad they did?"

"No." Darla's voice was flat. "Well, maybe. It's kind of a relief. I couldn't hide it any more, anyhow. It's so much worse than it used to be."

Something surfaced in Janeen's consciousness. "Brother Klassen's cupcakes," she said with finality. "That's what happened." Darla groaned and looked away. Janeen hardly heard her whispered affirmation.

One morning last year she'd gotten up even earlier than usual. It was Brother Klassen's birthday, and the class had agreed to surprise their seminary teacher. One girl offered to make a banner on her computer, and Janeen had volunteered to take cupcakes. It took a lot of effort to get up at five in the morning while Darla was still sleeping to mix and bake and ice a dozen and a half cupcakes. When Janeen lined them up evenly in a box to take them, it was with a feeling of accomplishment. They did look pretty, all white and clean with multicolored sprinkles, as if someone had scattered a snowdrift with bright flower petals.

Carefully, Janeen set the box on a corner of the counter. It was nearly six o'clock. She could hear Darla getting ready upstairs. Janeen ran to pile her books into a backpack and brush her hair one more time.

When their ride drove up, Janeen dashed to the kitchen to get the cupcakes, thinking that she would have to hold them carefully on her lap in the car. She put out her hands to pick up the box and was startled when it nearly flew upward. There was no weight in the box. The cupcakes were gone. A few red and yellow sprinkles lay in the corners of the otherwise empty cardboard container.

Incredulously, Janeen checked the cupboards, the fridge, even the dishwasher. Then she checked the fridge again, frantically shoving aside milk cartons and leftovers and margarine. Not there. When asked, Darla said innocently that she hadn't seen any cupcakes and turned to put on her jacket. No one else was up, Janeen knew. It had to have been Darla. An impatient honk broke the early morning stillness. The two girls locked eyes. Darla looked away and ran for the car. Janeen followed, slowly closing the door behind her, still confused and unbelieving. Why would Darla throw them out? she asked herself. Could Darla *really* be so mean? Why?

They still had the banner, anyway, and they all sang happy birthday. And maybe, as Brother Klassen had reassured Janeen, cupcakes were not the best thing to start the day with, after all. But Janeen was embarrassed at letting her classmates down and angry at Darla for hiding the cupcakes, or ruining them, or whatever she had done. Darla herself was absent for most of the class (she'd gone to the bathroom, Janeen now remembered), not wanting to face her sister, Janeen supposed. And Darla never answered any subsequent questions about the whole incident. It was almost as if those cupcakes had been an early morning dream; they'd never been baked and iced so carefully.

"I ate every one of them," Darla whispered dully. "I wanted to stop, Neener. But I just couldn't." She turned to face Janeen. "I'm sorry." Darla burst into fresh tears and buried her head in her hands. "What am I going to do, Neener? What am I going to do?"

Not quite sure of what she was doing, Janeen reached out and pulled Darla to her. She pulled Darla's head down onto her shoulder, as their mother had so often done when they were children. It seemed weird to Janeen at first. She hadn't held Darla for years and years. Not since they were little girls. But then it felt good, natural. The next part felt natural, too. Janeen began to rock Darla slowly, side to side, rubbing a hand up and down her back. Darla relaxed slowly, burying her face in Janeen's shoulder. Her muffled voice sobbed, "I wanted to tell you, so many times. But I was so ashamed."

"Sssh," Janeen soothed. "I know. It's all right. Sssh."

They sat like that, in the van under the pines; murmuring and whispering, unburdening and confessing. Their arms remained about one another. Warm tears fell from Darla's blue eyes and from Janeen's brown ones. The girls sniffled loudly, and wiped the trickles of mascara from their faces. All the while Janeen was praying, casting about for the right thing to say.

At last she found the courage. "Darla, look. There's got to be some kind of program, isn't there? Some kind of therapy?"

"I am not crazy." Darla stiffened.

Maybe not, a voice inside Janeen admonished, as she held Darla's wasted body in her arms like a broken doll. But you are definitely not normal.

Aloud, she soothed: "No, Darla. You're not crazy. But you said that you couldn't stop. And that's what's scary." Janeen tilted her head down and looked into Darla's fragile face. "You need help. You can't stay this miserable. And you're hurting yourself." Darla slumped into Janeen's shoulder again. "Okay?" Janeen coaxed. "Promise me, Gar."

Darla's tears were slower now, her breathing more even. Still, she clung to Janeen. "I'll think about it," she spoke into Janeen's neck.

Janeen looked over Darla's shoulder at her watch. They would have to get back soon. As it was, she would be grounded from driving for at least a month, for dragging Darla away with her and skipping church.

The girls huddled beneath the heavy limbs of the pines and mourned for childhood. It seemed to be fading that day into the gray winter light, brushing their faces softly as it left. The windshield began to fog up. A chill crept slowly into their hands and feet. From across the ridge they heard a siren's mournful wail, echoing Darla's cries. Now and then a cold gust would throw itself at the van, shaking it roughly.

At last, with a final sigh, Janeen straightened up. Sacrament meeting must be over. She felt very old. Not adult. Old. Oil of Olay old. She pushed the feeling aside. "Ready, Gar?" she asked, patting Darla's back as she slid back to her seat. Janeen's question hung in a light frost between them.

Darla sat up and rubbed her sleeves against her eyes, now completely devoid of makeup. She blew on her fingers and chafed her hands. Then she straightened up and exhaled noisily. "Ready, Neener! Hit the road." Janeen dug a piece of gum out of the console, offered it to her sister, and then found another for herself.

"Now this," Darla pronounced, "is decent gum. Wintergreen. Real sugar."

As they drove along Parkland Boulevard, Darla smoothed

her wild hair. She glanced into the side mirror. "I should get this stuff cut. I look like some kind of Beauty Culture experiment." She laughed and asked Janeen, "Hey, did you see Sister Thorne's hair today? Looked like she was wearing a bundt cake on her head!"

Janeen laughed too, feeling the heaviness inside her lift at the outrageous picture. Suddenly Darla grabbed her arm. "Let's go to Shear Magic tomorrow and get our hair buzzed off, both of us! It'd be fun, 'kay, Neen? Let's!" Darla was grinning with excitement at her idea.

Janeen grinned back. The van shuddered as she changed gears, and she laughed as they jolted forward. "Okay! A new look!" Janeen sobered for a moment as she eyed her sister. "A new start." She smiled again. "But I'll be grounded—you'll have to drive."

"Deal," was Darla's answer. She placed her hand on top of Janeen's on the stick shift and squeezed.

Neener felt Gar's hand, heard their mother's high, wild laugh in the poplar trees. The summer sun spilled warmth on their child-bright bodies, dappled with the poplars' shade. Outside the van, dry gray branches supplicated the clouded sky.

LOUISE: BABY SCHOOL

Louise Sullivan's eyebrows rose as the two teenagers bolted from the chapel. Some people raise their children any old way, without teaching them proper manners, she admitted sadly to herself. Girls that age have no excuse. Why, they must be old enough for Relief Society. But, Louise reminded herself, nothing would ruin this day for her. She had waited for this day for a long time.

Louise tucked her son Ethan's shirt in once again, loving the feel of his warm round belly as she did so. She straightened the cuffs of her crisp blouse and smoothed her already perfect, slightly graying brown hair. Louise had a round face, unremarkable save for the wide gray eyes that radiated faint lines about them. She wore a minimal amount of makeup, as always, preferring a simple, straightforward approach to her appearance.

She had judiciously chosen her wardrobe that morning, selecting something appropriate for both Primary President and Mother. Louise wore a tailored suit, its straight lines softened by small ruffles at the throat and cuffs of her pale rose blouse. She checked to make sure her necklace of heavy pink beads hung properly. The beads were the perfect touch, she thought. They were a favorite of hers, a gift from Riko when the two of them had taken that trip to California. Louise stole a glance up at Riko, sitting by herself on the stand.

Imagine! Riko as Relief Society president. How wonderful for her! Louise thought Riko's choice of a presidency was inspired. Rhonda Fitzpatrick was an obvious pick, capable and friendly. I never would have thought of Sharon Rasmussen, but Sharon will be a perfect homemaking counselor. And Virginia Thorne is precision itself. She has every family home evening lesson filed by category. Virginia will be a great help to Riko.

Louise and Riko shared a look, smiling at each other for a moment. I haven't seen much of Riko lately, Louise realized with a pang.

Louise's husband Bryce put his arm around her, and she shifted in toward him. The Sullivan family! Louise thrilled silently. A year after their son first came to them, the phrase still sounded new and untried.

She wondered vaguely if that smell was coming from Ethan.

Ethan pulled himself upright, bobbing up and down on her lap. "Ah!" he cooed. Suddenly intent on her necklace, Ethan's eyes widened as he slowly opened his mouth and took aim. Louise reached into her Primary bag for a distraction.

Louise had always carried in her heart a plan for her life. She would grow up and attend college. She laughed and told her friends that she just wasn't the type to get an "M.R.S." degree. She would finish school and become a teacher. She would enjoy the working life for a few years and then marry the perfect returned missionary. A few years later, they would begin to have a family, carefully planned and properly spaced. But lots of kids. Four, or maybe six.

She would stay home and be the kind of mother she'd had. She would have birthday parties and make cookies and bandage scrapes. She would teach the children to do the laundry and make lunches and feed the dog. She was convinced that she would settle disagreements firmly but nicely. She would be the perfect school volunteer mom, with her teaching experience. She would run the house smoothly and ensure there was always time for piano lessons and a place for the children to be creative. Maybe she'd teach again when they were in their teens.

"Ah!" Louise jumped at the unexpected attack. She looked around, smiling apologetically, and gently pried the jewelry from Ethan's clamped gums. She softly but firmly whispered, "No, Honey. Mommy's. No. No. Not Ethan's." She offered Baby Bunnykins and turned Ethan to the front. Ethan was a big boy for his age, solid and heavy on her lap. She rubbed his back fondly.

There had been a few significant changes to her rose-colored, imaginary home movies. Reality had reared its practical head.

Louise became engrossed in the challenge of teaching special ed. Just seeing one child grasp the meaning of a word and hold it like a glittering jewel gave her immense satisfaction. Busy and rewarding years slipped by. Louise couldn't seem to get interested in potential marriage candidates. She was used to her own company and found it difficult to get excited about dating "the unclaimed." Many of them seemed unclaimed for a reason, Louise and Riko sighed to one another. And Louise knew she wasn't going to marry someone who saw her only as a possible mother of his children. She wanted to truly love the man she would marry, and to respect him. She wanted a husband who would seek learning "even by study and also by faith." He had taken a good while coming, Louise thought now.

Louise and Riko had developed an easy companionship, a sisterhood, that sustained her during the rough times. Sometimes their thoughts would pour out in a voluble torrent over a pot of

chamomile tea. Sometimes they just sat and watched TV or
walked through Fish Creek Park. Their time together was sustaining and necessary.

Eventually, though, Louise admitted to herself that career
and girlfriends were little comfort when faced with the gurgling,
cooing bundles presented regularly by women years younger than
she was. It was time to marry and start a family. She was thirty-
nine years old.

She and Bryce Sullivan had married three years ago. Their
paths had crossed many times over the past decade, yet somehow
their timing had always been just a bit off. First he had gone back
down to BYU for two years, and then she had taken a job in
Edmonton. When she returned, he was off on a research trip to
England. Then they had studiously avoided each other because
it was clear to nearly every female in the ward that they should
get together.

Ethan squirmed around once more and immediately located
the object of his desire. Louise's necklace became slick with drool
as he gurgled his unbounded satisfaction. Louise sighed. "No,
Ethan." She removed it once more and retrieved the scorned
bunny.

When she and Bryce finally did start dating, each knew the
other was actively looking for a marriage partner. There was no
coy flirtation and very little beating around the bush. Their courtship had lasted exactly three months. It was an easy, friendly,
happy time of frank sharing and much give and take. Bryce had
openly admired her no-nonsense capability, and she appreciated
his intellect and analytical manner. She had grown to love and
appreciate Bryce in a way she felt no teenager could ever love and
appreciate a sweetheart. He expressed his desire to share eternity
with her, and they prayed together, seeking the confirmation that

came quietly and surely. And when they announced their forthcoming wedding, each of the previously mentioned good sisters of
the ward felt obliged to take credit for "knowing it all along."

She and Bryce wanted to start a family as soon as possible,
and they agreed to try for a pregnancy right away. Neither had
any doubt that it would happen. They were both healthy.
Certainly she was older than most first-time mothers, but Louise
saw her position as a Primary counselor and her years of teaching
as excellent qualifications for parenting. Surely Heavenly Father
would bless them soon.

Each month followed a pattern of hope, certainty, excitement, uncertainty, and then inevitably, disappointment. Each
month she had been dismayed at the persistence of her menstrual
cycle. She longed to feel a child grow within her, to feel her
breasts swell in anticipation and preparation. She hugged herself
tightly, wishing for all the world that she could cradle her own
child, hers and Bryce's.

They were both avid readers, and they devoured everything
they could find on the subject of infertility. Was it his fault? Hers?
Each secretly blamed the other, but no accusations were made.
They had gone around in circles that way for months. They
debated heatedly about in vitro fertilization. ("Harvesting eggs?"
Louise was incredulous. She had a sudden mental picture of doc-
tors in overalls with bandannas on their faces, prepared for the
harvest.) Her time was running out. Couples waited for years to
get into the infertility program at the university hospital. She did
not want to totter to her child's high school graduation, cane in
hand. Even if they could somehow get in sooner, the attempts
could well prove unsuccessful, setting them back further.

Riko, ever faithful, cheered from the sidelines. She found
funny stickers to put on her friend's temperature charts and knew

better than to call on certain well-timed evenings of the month. She was always a phone call away when Louise's period came yet again. And she encouraged Louise when it became clear that more drastic measures would have to be taken.

Louise's son began to bat her firmly with Baby Bunnykins. This was having a detrimental effect on her coiffure, she was sure. She lowered his chubby arm and turned him to the front once more, hissing that he had better stop it.

Bryce had been enthusiastic about adopting a child, perhaps because he had an adopted cousin. Yet, Louise had felt very insecure about adoption. They would not know the child's background. "What if he or she develops serious problems as a teenager, and the problem stems from a stressful prenatal environment? There are studies that show that is a big factor. Can we take that chance?" she asked him. "What if the child's mother decides to take it away again? What if it is just so different from us that it feels alienated? It might not look anything like us. We would have to explain to him or her about the adoption someday. The child would likely take it very hard."

Bryce had rightly pointed out that, stacked up against the possibility of having a family, her arguments were flimsy. He gently stated that she was throwing up obstacles because she was defensive about her inability to have a child. She had to admit that he was right. But still, raising the offspring of another woman's womb as her own . . . it wasn't natural. Not at all what she'd planned. Riko had rolled her eyes in an uncharacteristically dramatic fashion. "What's the difference? You know you would love it just as much. You couldn't hold back if you tried."

Ethan, at his tender age, had learned the advantage of persistence. This would be a great help in his future endeavors, his mother was sure, but right now it was decidedly inconvenient. She handed him over to his father.

Somewhat reluctantly, she had agreed to go to LDS Social Services but only to "explore the options."

The Sullivans had explained their position carefully to the good brother there. They wanted to find out what was involved in the adoption process, they said, but Louise made it clear that they would not make any commitments.

When the forms came in the mail, Louise began to picture a tiny baby being handed to her, an eternal gift. Perhaps only the first of a larger family. Her resistance began to ebb. The impossible suddenly seemed possible. She grew enthusiastic and hopeful. She would love the baby so much, she told herself, that it would never have a chance to doubt that it belonged with them.

And suddenly there was so much to do. Letters to the bishop, references, interviews, home visits. Louise read everything she could on the neonatal environment, infant stimulation, and IQ and heredity. She had a fat file of clippings from newspapers and parenting magazines. Researching and reading was all she could do to avoid the agony of waiting. That, and prayer.

In Alberta, they learned, a birth mother who has chosen to give up her child through a church-sponsored private adoption has the opportunity to choose the new parents. She examines files on several prospective families and then makes her choice. Louise and Bryce fervently prayed that one of the young mothers would pick their profile from among the four or five she read. Louise grew anxious at the thought that her happiness rested in a manila folder in the nail-bitten hands of a teenager. Would the girl know that Louise and Bryce would make a good, no, the best family for her child?

And the prayed-for bounty was granted. They were informed

that they would meet with a teenaged mother, prepared to bestow on them her twin girls. Louise could barely contain her excitement. "At last!" she bubbled to friends and colleagues, "And twins, too!" It seemed the Sullivans' long frustration was finally going to end in a froth of ribbon and lace.

Louise made arrangements to take a maternity leave from work. Bryce painted a bedroom pink and installed darling wicker bassinets with eyelet flounces. Louise spent an entire long weekend preparing the room for the royal princesses. When Riko saw it, she smiled her wide, silent smile at Louise's excess. "What did you do, clean out Babies R Us?" Every puff, every bow and ruffle and heart, every tiny flower, had been arranged just so. There was a nursery monitor, a tape recorder releasing a flowing stream of Mozart, and a smiling face hung above each bassinet. Riko declared that it simply would not be complete without a mobile. Her eyes brimmed as she presented Louise with clouds of recumbent angels that gently rotated to a built-in music box. Louise hung it from the ceiling, and the two friends stood in the pink room as it played, holding each other and crying.

Louise had lain awake for the next several nights, anticipating the two tiny girls, the sweet little dresses she would buy, and the myriad details that would need to be attended to. One night as she began to drift into sleep, she realized with a start that she hardly knew a thing about inoculation. It would be awful if they caught something, she thought. She would call the health unit first thing in the morning.

What about feedings? Should she feed them both at the same time? she wondered. Then Bryce would have to help too, and that wouldn't work. One at a time, then, Louise decided. But she would be feeding all day! There was a Twins Club in the city. She must find out about that. It can't be too difficult to raise twins, Louise speculated. You just have to have extra of everything.

Ethan leaned across from Bryce's lap. Baby Bunnykins flew into the pew behind Louise. Lenora Bertram picked it up and handed it to Ethan, poking it into his fat belly. Ethan liked this game. He cooed and gurgled his appreciation. Sister Bertram whispered a few words in baby talk and handed him the rabbit. Louise turned and smiled at Lenora. Such a nice person, she thought. Louise had heard rumors about Lenora's health. I wonder if she is as ill as they say? She made a mental note to get to know her better.

Hoping to prolong the game, Ethan pitched Baby Bunnykins back. It was happily returned and then flung again. This time when it was returned, Louise made sure it went into the diaper bag. Enough is enough. Ethan then attempted to use her necklace as a rope to pull himself to a standing position. She winced as she leaned forward to keep the necklace from snapping.

She knew who was boss. She forcibly removed the shining wet beads from the grasp of little hands and mouth. She lifted Ethan from Bryce's hands, straightened, and began to jiggle her son lightly. Her kiss left a trace of coral lipstick that she absently rubbed with her thumb.

The twins! Night and day she had thought of little except the babies. Every child she saw at the school reminded her of qualities she should or should not cultivate in the girls. In sacrament meeting she watched the families around her and shook her head imperceptibly, determined that her children would behave appropriately in church. Her children would have respect for the Lord and his house. No crayons, no cereal. They would learn from the beginning.

Louise and Bryce waited anxiously for the arrival of "their"

girls. They knew the babies were due any day. When at last
Brother Thompson called, though, their excitement was quickly
quashed by the tone of his voice. Brother Thompson sounded
somber and apologetic, and he needed to see them as soon as possible. Bryce left work early that afternoon to pick up his wife.
They drove the half hour to LDS Social Services in silence, each
occasionally stealing a glance at the other. As they entered the
office with Brother Thompson, Louise noticed that his genial,
open face was suffused with tenderness. Her heart sank in fearful
premonition. When she and Bryce sat down, he pulled up a chair
across from them.

"Occasionally, despite our efforts to be fair to everyone,
things don't work out quite the way we intended. But they seem
to work out the way our Father in Heaven wants them to." He
looked downward and ran a hand over his thick, graying hair as
he searched for words. Instinctively, Louise and Bryce grasped
each other's hands. Louise held her breath and felt her pulse push
at her fingertips and toes. She held on to Bryce as if he represented
those baby girls, her slipping chance at motherhood and a family.

Brother Thompson raised his head. "There's a hitch in our
plans." He leaned forward. His warm, golden brown eyes gazed
directly into Louise's. "The mother has decided to keep the girls.
Her parents will help her . . . I'm sorry, Louise, Bryce."

Louise fought the impulse to shout angrily at Brother
Thompson. Covering her face, she gritted her teeth. She felt
defeated and, most of all, furious. She knew she should be happy
for the mother, happy that she could care for her children, that
she wanted them. But she had taken away what Louise already
thought of as her and Bryce's family. Even as Brother Thompson's
hushed voice rose in a prayer to plead for understanding and comfort, Louise inwardly protested that she and Bryce would have

done a better job of rearing those girls. They had the money, the education, the desire to make a wonderful home. It was so unfair! Heavenly Father must see that!

In the weeks that followed, she continued to soothe her raging, aching heart with prayers, and she grew calmer. Louise threw herself back into caring for "her" handicapped schoolchildren. She pulled the shades in the nursery and closed the door. She would not talk about it, even to Riko. The pink room languished, unused, at the end of the hall. The bassinets lay empty and cool, and clouds of angels stirred restlessly in the darkness.

They had just begun to adjust once more to the familiar ache of childlessness, when they received another call. Brother Thompson could hardly contain his excitement over the phone. And then Ethan bounced into their lives.

He was bouncing still, as he wrapped both chubby fists in his mother's necklace and noisily savored the slippery feel of the beads sliding through his inquisitive mouth. Louise suppressed a groan, but she knew who was really boss. With difficulty, because her child was attached like a plump pendant, she ducked out of the necklace. She pursed her lips as she smoothed her hair. Ethan burbled and spit and chomped with an abandon that was slightly alarming.

Louise had been so afraid to hope. Even as they'd entered the brightly lit, barren hospital, she hadn't allowed herself to believe it. How could this stark place yield life? The elevator was so slow! As the doors opened to Maternity, Bryce had to give her a gentle tug. LDS Social Services had required her to write a letter to the birth mother. Louise's hands trembled as she drew it from her purse. Over her arm hung a carefully chosen blue blanket, a tiny train running around the satin borders.

They stepped out into the too-bright hallway. It seemed a

long time until their echoing footsteps brought them to the nursery window. They peered at the unbelievably small, helpless humans that squinted at life, their fists and feet wriggling in the white flannel blankets. Was he in there? Which one was he? Louise clutched the letter tightly as she searched for some sign, some clue among the bassinets.

She felt a tap on her shoulder and turned to greet Brother Thompson. The smile that lit his face as he shook their hands nearly brought Louise to her knees. It was going to happen. It was really going to happen this time. She would leave this sterile place a mother.

She was shaking as they followed Brother Thompson. He knocked softly and then opened a wide door. Seated in a stark room, a girl, barely sixteen, cradled a bundle wrapped in a crocheted blanket. She had tears in her dark-ringed eyes as she looked up at them. She greeted them with a sad little smile touched with lip gloss. Her peach-colored terry housecoat hung on her thin frame. Dark hair flowed in smoothly brushed curls about her face. She had prepared herself to say good-bye to her boy. Louise noticed that she held a letter as well. Louise's eyes settled on the baby in the girl's arms, and at once she had to see him.

Her arms reached out yearningly, pulling her across the floor. She thought her heart would explode with aching. It seemed like an eternity before she could scoop up their sweet, their own, baby boy. She held him then, with Bryce at her side, staring into the dark, half-opened eyes surrounded by delicate lashes. She touched the translucent skin and marveled at the fine silky strands of hair. Her hand rested on the soft spot of his skull, feeling the warm pulse vibrating there. Several silent minutes went by as she and Bryce drank in the presence of their son.

Suddenly, Louise bent and held his young mother to her. "Thank you, oh thank you!" Louise kissed the top of the teenager's dark head. Then she added in a choked whisper, "Bless you."

The girl squeezed Louise's arm. "Just love him," she said, in a hushed, tearful voice. She noticed the blue blanket over Louise's arm. "Please," she whispered hesitantly, "can he keep this blanket?" She tugged at the afghan wrapped around her son. "I made it just for him. I want him to have something from me."

"Of course! Of course, he will keep it . . . And I will tell him you made it for him. I promise." They exchanged letters. Both would treasure these pieces of paper for the rest of their lives.

"We've already named him," Bryce smiled through his tears. "His name is Ethan."

Upon hearing that, the young mother's eyes widened. She trembled as she whispered. "Ethan! That's his name, what I called him!" The tears overflowed as she smiled crookedly. "Now I know that you were meant to be his parents." She gazed raptly at the baby, so recently brought to this world from her pain-racked, small body. Biting her lip, she stroked his fist, too overcome to say more.

The hallway resonated with its morning routine . . . hurrying footsteps, keys jingling, nurses calling to one another, orderlies whistling . . . Sounds floated by, unheard by the hushed gathering. Unmoving, they formed a tableau of wonder-struck joy and wrenching pain. At last Brother Thompson stepped forward, indicating that they should leave.

Turning to the girl in the faded robe, Louise promised to send pictures until Ethan's first birthday, as was permitted. After a year, the adoption would at last be finalized, and Ethan could be blessed by his adoptive father. Then, they had agreed, they would go to the temple; and Ethan would be sealed to them, forming an eternal bond.

"Can I hold him once more, to say good-bye?" the girl asked. Gently, she took the baby in his blanket, created during long months of pregnancy. She hugged him to the body from which he had entered the world and then bent her face to his. "Ethan, I love you. I will always love you." She kissed him tenderly. "Good-bye," she whispered. She turned her head away as she handed him to his new mother. She did not watch as the Sullivans, sobbing, left the room with her child. Brother Thompson saw them out and then reentered the room. They heard his voice, low and comforting, from the other side of the door.

Now, the year past, Louise silently thanked that frail girl. When Mother's Day had come, Bryce had given her two roses. He explained to Louise that one was for her and one was for the young mother who had placed Ethan in their care. Louise hoped the girl was happy. Many times she offered up a prayer for that thin, dark-eyed stranger, and she now did so again. "I will thank her when I bear my testimony today," Louise thought. "It is the very least I can do. She has given us so much."

Louise kissed the boy who was now dropping her favorite necklace into the hymnbook shelf. Picking it up. Dropping it into the hymnbook shelf. Picking it up. Here was a baby that could not be more loved and fussed over and cosseted! A child that held her very heart in those dimpled and damp fists.

A child that demanded the best she had to give. She had never faced a challenge like this before, in all her years of teaching. In the twelve months since that teenager had given up her baby, he had introduced them to a previously undreamed-of world. A world of colic and sleepless nights. Of projectile vomiting and rectal thermometers. A world often dominated by sore, unsoothable gums. A world of ointments and diaper rash. And this world had proved to be a very cluttered and untidy one, at that. Many times as Louise rose early to feed Ethan, she would look about her once-immaculate home and wonder what, exactly, had happened. One small child could surely not account for this much disarray.

At times she wished that women like her could just go to a Baby School and get a degree in Child Management. She had wryly voiced this sentiment to Glenda Klassen once, who had six or seven children of her own, and Glenda had laughed. "No one ever graduates from this program," Glenda told her, "because the qualifications keep changing!" Louise had gained a new respect for Glenda Klassen.

Ethan smiled at her and granted her his greatest expression of love. He softly bit her nose. Louise's eyes misted at this sudden display of affection. She fished for a tissue in her purse.

Seeing the Aladdin's cave of his mother's purse, Ethan quickly discarded the necklace. Louise sat resigned as he studied the contents of this newfound trove. Keys. Into the mouth. A pen. Apparently he didn't like the taste. A grocery receipt merited oral attention. Louise dabbed surreptitiously at her nose with the back of her hand.

As she scooped soggy wads of paper from her son's mouth, she reached for the bottle of apple juice from the diaper bag beside her and put her purse and the Primary bag on the floor. Peace at last. Ethan's hard, warm head rested against her shoulder. Soft, contented throat songs rose gently in her praise. She stroked his head. Yes, Ethan demanded a lot.

In return Ethan gave them only one thing. Life-sustaining unconditional love.

I guess that's why people have kids, sighed Louise. I suppose you don't need Baby School to comprehend that.

Today, her son had been blessed. Our boy, the Sullivan boy, Louise thought happily. Bryce had cradled Ethan and pronounced a blessing. A life of fullness and goodness . . . a mission when Ethan grew up . . . strength and righteousness to be with him always . . . and a family that loved him past all expression.

Ethan chewed on the nipple of the bottle and blew her a lovely, apple-juice-laden raspberry. "Ma! Ba da. Ah!" he exclaimed. Louise felt a gentle hand on her shoulder. Lenora Bertram leaned forward, smiling, and handed her a tissue. Louise accepted it gratefully. She smiled at her wet, gurgling son as she wiped her cheek.

VIRGINIA: RAPUNZEL'S TREASURE

Virginia Thorne had sat stiffly through the blessing of the Sullivan baby. She could not concentrate this morning. Not on the baby or his father's reassuring words. Virginia was worrying about her hair. She had done it specially for the sustaining today. She'd wanted it to be perfect. Her husband, Robert, had mentioned that it looked different this morning. He had seemed offhand enough, but she wondered if it was his gentle way of suggesting there was something wrong with it. It had taken her ages to do the intricate braid that wove her long, thick hair into a crown around her head, with the end coiled neatly into the braid. You couldn't tell where it began or ended, and that was the charm of it, really. It was very Victorian looking. She had thought it rather elegant.

But he had said . . . she glanced about her. Of course no one else had the same sort of hairstyle. That was to be expected. It seemed to her that Mormon women were just too complacent when it came to their appearance. Look at Lenora Bertram sitting over near the Sullivans, with her no-nonsense helmet of hair. She felt a twinge of guilt at judging Lenora. Lenora actually did look far more stylish than usual today, and considering what she was going through, that was amazing, Virginia thought.

Virginia fancied that she was somewhat of a fashion stand-out in this small ward. Italian leather purses, English overcoats, the feminine touches of Laura Ashley and Jessica McClintock. People expected it of her, she had come to believe. She would never let herself be seen without makeup and earrings, and even in jeans she was soft and romantic looking with her mane of hair and ruffled blouses.

You had to have the figure to dress beautifully, Virginia told herself. It called for a strict diet. She scolded herself again. She had overdone it last night, and that must be corrected. She would manage herself more carefully, she vowed. She decided the bread and water of the sacrament would have to be enough to last her until tomorrow. She hadn't fasted anyway, she reasoned, so this would be all right. She was sure that even Robert would have to agree. She closed her eyes as one of the young men spoke into the microphone, "O God, the Eternal Father . . . "

She'd had only a few hours of sleep last night. She'd had the dream again. She was high in a tower, longing to escape, and then an ugly bird swooped in, screaming and clawing and attacking her head. Its awful mouth stretched wide, and its eyes were terrifying in their ferocity.

Virginia had awakened suddenly, her heart pounding. For a long time she lay and listened to Robert's slow, even breathing. Then there were the usual Sunday morning duties—putting supper in the Crock-Pot, making sure the girls' dresses were pressed and their crinolines ready, and of course, her manicure. It had taken longer than usual this morning: her hands were still shaking slightly from that horrible dream. And then she had done the girls' hair and her own. She had fussed and fussed with hers, trying to follow the instructions in the book to the letter. Styling her hair had taken nearly an hour, but Virginia wanted it to be just perfect.

What had Robert meant, "unusual"? she wondered. She thought he'd sounded rather flip. Was he laughing at her? No, she assured herself, he wouldn't do that. Would he? She stretched out a manicured hand and daintily took a morsel of bread from the tray. She passed it on to Robert.

Virginia was sure some of the women here looked at her with envy. She didn't doubt that she was better dressed, more neatly groomed than most. She had felt the admiring glances as she stood when the presidency was sustained. Virginia wondered if she were prettiest. Rhonda was elegant, sleek looking . . . but she was well into middle age. Sharon, Virginia shrugged, was just Sharon. She didn't seem to care much about how she looked. Of course, Riko was very lovely, always gracious and self-possessed, a perfect choice for Relief Society president—so long as her counselors had some experience with families, which they did.

Of her own abilities as Relief Society secretary, Virginia was fairly certain, although she had never filled the position before. Virginia had always viewed the secretary as a mere functionary of the more important positions. When Riko explained it, though, it became clear the Relief Society secretary was much more. Really a third counselor. Riko needed someone with an eye for detail, "to handle the nuts-and-bolts stuff—attendance, budget, visiting teaching stats . . . ," Riko had told her.

Virginia had done some secretarial work before she'd had the girls. There would be a lot of work involved, but she was determined to do a good job of it. She was nothing if not organized, she told herself firmly.

Virginia's gaze rested upon Riko again, who sat with her eyes closed as the second sacrament prayer was spoken. She is a lovely woman. But it's more than her face and clothing, Virginia thought, vainly trying to find a name for the kind of beauty she saw in Riko. It eluded her.

Virginia's father had always lined up his little girls before church—Virginia, Nanette, Jennifer, and Christina—to see who was prettiest that day. Virginia felt again the cramping in the pit of her stomach as her father's steely eyes flicked over his daughters in assessment. Usually Nanette was prettiest, but sometimes, only occasionally, the honor was Virginia's. If she had a beautiful new dress, say, or had put a wide satin bow in her hair.

Virginia lifted a cup of clear water from the silver tray and passed it on.

She drifted into a hazy sunlit memory. She had been about seven, she guessed, and it was late summer.

Virginia sat on the stiff maroon leather chair, wondering why people came to this place. Her mother was talking to a nice-looking man who wore a pale blue shirt like the dentist wore. He smiled at Virginia and at her three little sisters lined up across from her like dolls in a shop window. Something about the smile made Virginia wary. It was the kind of smile her father made just before he explained that she was a big girl and if she continued to cry, she would be spanked, hard.

She wiggled in the chair and discovered that this caused the chair to move from side to side. Seeing it, Nanette ran over and began to slowly spin the chair, giggling at the surprised look on Jennifer's and Christina's faces. Virginia looked down at her sister. Nanette was so pretty, everyone said. And they were right. Nanette had the pert nose, the heart-shaped face, that caused adults to glance at her a second, even a third, time to take in the slightly slanted blue eyes, the sprinkle of freckles, and the smile that only hinted at sauciness. Virginia felt a twinge of envy as she looked at her sister. She refused to smile.

Mother and the man were still talking: they had their backs turned to the girls.

Nanette took this as a cue to spin the chair faster, to see if that would make Virginia smile, or, even better, yell at her. It was fun to make Virginia mad, even if she did get in trouble.

Resolutely, Virginia kept her eyes in front of her, seeing a wildly careening room of faded colors and unfamiliar posters whizzing around her. Then she caught sight of herself in the mirror, and she smiled.

When she spun, her hair flew out behind her in a glorious, shining curtain of gold. It waved about her face like Rapunzel's treasure, a cascade of softly curling sunshine. She began to laugh. She had a halo! She was the most beautiful little girl in the world. Even Nanette didn't have hair like hers!

"Girls! Stop that right now. That's no way to behave!" Mother's sharp words cut through the heavy afternoon air of the shop, causing Nanette to give one final shove and then scamper to the wall beside her sisters. They knew Mother meant business. Mother always meant business, and she always told them she meant business.

"I mean business! Can't I even take you out in public without being embarrassed by your behavior?"

They did not answer. They were not supposed to.

Chastened, Virginia gazed at her hands, clutching the worn doll she held there. She slowly raised her eyes and looked at her reflection once more. Virginia was flushed and slightly fuzzy looking, as if she'd been lightly dusted with a fine iridescent powder. Strands of gold looped this way and that, giving her an appearance that was fairylike, appealing. She pushed a few tendrils of hair from her face and smiled at herself.

The man was standing behind her. He tied a dark plastic cape around her neck.

He took out a comb.

"Mother, why are we here?" Virginia squeezed her doll. "What is the comb for?" She tried to ask politely. She knew her mother did not like to be annoyed. But she felt a hole open up inside her stomach, like the time she climbed all the way to the top of the garage and then looked down and saw the awfulness of her height. "What is he doing?"

"The comb is to comb your hair, Virginia. That is usually what combs are for. Now sit there like a good girl. You are the oldest, and you must go first. Not another word."

The man lifted the comb and slowly worked it through Virginia's hair. She didn't like the way he touched it. He stroked it gently, running the soft waves through his fingers. He seemed to take a long time to comb her hair. What was he doing? Was this a contest? Once Mother had taken her to a contest at a shopping center. They were looking for "Little Miss Whiteoaks." It was a modeling opportunity, her mother said. Nanette wasn't old enough, so Virginia was the one who got a new dress, with a pink, broad-brimmed hat and matching lace-trimmed gloves. Mother made her practice smiling and curtsying and saying "Thank you. My name is Virginia Sinclair." Mother made her do it over and over again, until she began to worry about every detail of her short speech, every small nuance of her walk, the terrifying unfamiliarity of a curtsy. When the day came, Mother left all the other girls with Father and took only Virginia. All the way to the shopping center she coached her daughter on the right way to speak, stand, turn, walk, curtsy, smile . . . "and for goodness' sake did you not brush your teeth, Virginia? I told you three times if you lose because of your teeth I don't know what I'll do I work my fingers to the bone to give you everything I never had give you opportunities to make something of yourself and what do you do throw it in my face you are just disgraceful and very very ungrateful you have to make the most of yourself you are not the prettiest not like Nanette but still you have bone structure and . . . "

Virginia wet her pants. Patricia Sue Scott was Little Miss Whiteoaks, and she got the gift certificate, the Barbie gift pack, and the spring ensemble from Bopeep's.

Virginia got a lecture.

Now, as she felt the man running his fingers through her hair, she wondered what she should do. She smiled at his reflection weakly, but he did not meet her gaze, entranced as he was by the golden fibers he held. He murmured softly. She could feel the cool tips of his fingers on the back of her neck. His breath was warm and smelled of spearmint gum. Virginia squirmed uncomfortably.

"Lovely, lovely. Such a shame. Well, I suppose you know best, Mom!"

Nobody ever called her Mom, thought Virginia. Not even Christina.

With a big, phoney smile, the man said, "Gonna make you look just like a movie star, honey." He winked broadly.

The hole in Virginia's stomach grew larger and deeper. She stared at her face in the mirror, wondering why she should want to look like a movie star. She stared into her own eyes, willing them to tell her what the man and her mother were going to do.

"Tsst tsst tsst." She felt scissors touch her neck icily.

The horror of what was happening dawned on Virginia in a single awful moment. "NO! Mother! Mother! He's cutting it all

off! No!" Virginia twisted as she tried to get down off the horrible chair. She felt firm hands on her shoulders. Her mother's
hands.

"Darling, it will look lovely. It is such a bother to comb out
all the time. You will see. Now stop being such a baby. If you can't
behave like a young lady, I will take privileges away. I hope I
don't have to tell your father that you have misbehaved today.
Do you understand, Virginia?" Mother's tone was cool and steely.
"Virginia, answer me. Do you understand?"

Virginia made a great effort to stop her chest from heaving
in and out. She tried hard to push the tears back inside her eyes.
She grimaced as she tried to force her bottom lip from curling
and wrenching downward in grief. But her throat! Her throat
hurt as she gulped her shock and anger down, down inside. It
might come out anytime; she had to push it in where Mother
wouldn't see it. She had to clench her teeth and close her eyes
and pretend that she and her dolly were home, in the playhouse,
in bed, anywhere!

"Virginia! Answer me!" Mother demanded, her hands were
pushing on the little girl's shoulders, the nails insistent on the
soft pale flesh beneath the ugly cape.

"Y-y-yes, Mother. I—I understand," Virginia choked at last.

"There's my girl. Just sit still and let the barber do what he
needs to do. I was hoping for more of a pixie style," she added to
the man, gesturing with immaculately manicured hands.

And so all Virginia could do was hold Dolly tight and watch
silently as Rapunzel lost her treasure, lock by precious lock. In
the mirror she saw Nanette's usually animated face. Now it was
still and tight. The bright blue eyes were wide with trepidation.
She would be next.

Nanette, and Jennifer, and Christina. Pixie cuts for all. So cute and so easy to care for, perfect for the summer, your father will wonder who these lovely little Parisiennes are and my just think how envious all your little friends will be I'm sure they'll all want to look just like you because it's really the latest style and everyone absolutely everyone says short hair is really the way to go . . .

It was in a box. A lovely pale lavender box with cream-colored roses embossed on the lid. "Cavendish's," the silver lettering delicately announced. "Finer dresses for finer ladies."

She could lift it up, sift it through her fingers. She could sit in front of the sunlight and let it play a music of light on the golden strands. She could hold it up in front of the mirror and pretend that she was the prettiest, that no one would look at Nanette because of Virginia's waterfall of wild beauty.

She cried, though, because when she put it back under the bed, she felt the cool air on the back of her neck, like an evil spell cast by Rapunzel's wicked captor.

Virginia took out the box of severed hair every few days. It would grow back. It had grown an inch already. In two months. She knew that an inch was not very much. An inch was hardly anything.

Nanette looked cute, elfin and poised with a pixie cut. Jennifer and Christina didn't care. At least they didn't have food in their hair all the time, as Mother often remarked.

And one day, the box was gone.

"It was clutter." said Mother. "You know how I can't stand clutter. And it's not right to have it lying around. Things could nest in it, or grow in it. It's very unsanitary."

It really was gone, reflected Virginia as she gazed in the mirror at the worried round face, the sorrowful gray-blue eyes. It was gone. Rapunzel was just a fairy tale, after all. And they never, never come true. At least, that's what Mother said.

With a start, Virginia came suddenly to reality. Her husband had taken her hand in his. He was smiling warmly at her. "You look so beautiful today, Virginia! What are you thinking about? Pretty serious, by the look of it," he whispered tenderly.

Her hair was all right, then! She made an effort to erase the crease between her brows. Mother used to put tape on that spot to make her own wrinkles go away. Did it help? She tried to think of her mother's face, and recalled deep lines, angry lines. No, she would not bother trying the tape. Virginia smiled. "Nothing, sweetheart. Just remembering something my sisters and I did once." She mentally added, Or rather, what Mother did to us.

The bishop stood and began to bear his testimony. Soon he would turn the meeting over to members of the ward to do the same.

Annoyed by the shifting of Jessica Rose beside her, she turned to her daughter. "Jessica Rose, please. Can't I take you out without you embarrassing me?" She motioned to her other child, sitting on Robert's lap. "Ashleigh Anne is not squirming, and she is younger than you. You must sit still. Read your book if you have to, but stop wiggling!"

Jessica Rose's lip trembled. Virginia laid a hand on her leg, wanting to squeeze hard, to force her to hold still. She suddenly had a vision of perfectly manicured nails, fingers on her shoulders, delicate gestures in the barber's direction. Virginia gently patted her daughter's leg. "I know this is a long time for you, Jessie," she whispered. "Why don't you rest your head against me? Close your eyes and think about what you'd like to do when Auntie Nan and your cousins come next week. Think of all the fun you'll have!" There would be no beauty contests for Jessica Rose.

Virginia lifted her hand and stroked her daughter's shining hair. Her hand was beautifully shaped, the nails perfect, the rings sparkling. It was tense as she touched her daughter's head. Jessica Rose must not grow up to be like this, she thought. I owe her more than that. She sent a silent prayer to heaven.

Virginia buried her face in Jessica Rose's curls. "Soon, honey. It will be over soon." Grateful for this child—for both her children—grateful for Robert and his understanding, Virginia was filled with a surge of love. Tears stung her eyes.

A skinny, freckled deacon perched on the edge of a pew at the front of the chapel. He clutched a microphone tightly, the cord coiling about his feet, his eyes scanning the ward restlessly. The deacon was anxious to present the mike to anyone who wished to stand and speak.

Virginia got to her feet, her head high, stretching her arm before her. She patted her daughter's shoulder fondly and then took the mike from the boy's hand.

LENORA: DANCING WITH DEATH

Lenora Bertram struggled to contain her emotion. *I must get through this without breaking down!* she scolded herself. She stood taller. Gripping the back of the pew ahead of her, trying to breathe deeply, she looked up and spoke into the microphone once more. She could feel her family's presence behind her, their support shoring her flagging strength.

Louise Sullivan, sitting ahead of her, turned to place a hand on Lenora's, squeezing it gently. Louise and Bryce had followed Virginia Thorne's lead, bearing testimonies full of hope and happiness. Louise's eyes were deep with concern as she looked at Lenora. Lenora smiled weakly at her, and continued bearing her testimony.

" . . . and after we moved here from Ontario, I got involved in what's known as 'Palliative Care.' Care for the dying. I took a course through Calgary General. We visit the terminally ill and help ease their minds about what lies ahead for them. We know what lies beyond that veil, but some of those people aren't so lucky." She paused. "I'm not sure exactly why Heavenly Father chose to spare me, but I feel as if I need to tell people that when you're really, really there, looking death in the face, it doesn't have to be scary and sad and awful." She swallowed hard. "We know, as members of the Church, that there is much more beyond this world, and I want to share that with those people. I want to comfort them as I was comforted." Lenora lost the battle and began to weep softly.

Two weeks ago she had sat across from Reg. He hadn't much longer now. Reg was thirty-three, a former biker. Inky snakes wound their way up his now shriveled arms, the tattooed remains of his past. Their heads slumbered beneath the hospital gown. "I called my dad and mom today. They don't want to talk about it."

His flat voice did not conceal his pain. Reg's family had not seen him since he was diagnosed with the AIDS virus two years ago. His eyes welled up with tears. "I'm afraid, Lenora."

Lenora took both his hands in hers. "Reg, I've been there."

"No you haven't!" he insisted. "You haven't been here!" He pointed at his thin chest. "I like you, Lenora. You really try. But no white-bread Mormon lady can tell me she knows what I'm going through."

She replied quietly, squeezing Reg's hands gently. "I know. You're right. But I didn't mean there." She looked into his red-rimmed eyes. "I meant . . . there. Where you're going. I've been there. And it was . . . peaceful, and wonderful. Serene."

Reg's watery eyes widened. "Holy . . . " He stopped himself. "Lenora, you never told me that! Was that . . . that time before you got the new ticker?" He gripped her hands tighter now. "Tell me about it, Lenora. I always wondered, but I never talked to anyone who'd really . . . Was it beautiful?"

She smiled. "You won't hurt any more, Reg. And yes, it's more than beautiful . . . it's better than any place you've ever been." She paused. "It was hard to leave, once I'd been there.

They said I had to come back, and it made me kind of mad." She chuckled and then became serious. "It hurt a lot to come back. But still, it's harder to let go . . . " She rubbed the back of Reg's pale hand with her thumb and gazed beyond him, through the window. Skeletal trees in thin shrouds of frost clawed toward the sky. She did not tell Reg that she was afraid too. Afraid that she was running out of time.

Lenora continued bearing her testimony, looking directly at various members of the ward who turned to her attentively. "I want to tell my family how much I love and appreciate them, and I know that each one of my children will go far in life. Each one of them is so very, very special. And I want to tell my husband how grateful I am for his support and his unconditional love." In her mind's eye, Lenora saw again his anxious face as she swam up from anesthetic. He had spent many hours praying in barren hospital rooms. "He is truly the best husband I could ever wish for. I am so grateful he is my eternal companion."

Her voice shook as she ended her testimony simply and humbly and sat once more. She closed her eyes, remembering Reg. His ashes now filled a metal urn in an echoing mausoleum. She hoped her friend was happy now, free of his pain. She prayed that, this time, he would accept the gospel. It had brought her so much!

Lenora felt Dan's arm around her shoulders as she bent forward and rested her head on the pew before her. He squeezed her reassuringly. There was a slight note of worry in his voice as he asked, "Lennie, are you all right?"

Lenora almost didn't hear him. Her heart was so full of her blessings, it seemed it was going to burst. It beat harder and faster as she fought to gain control. Her heart played a relentless, accelerating drum beat that threatened to suffocate her. Lenora wished it would just calm down. She had thought many times that the young man who had owned this heart before her must have been very excitable indeed. Lately the heart had leapt and danced and jumped in a frenzy of joy that left Lenora exhausted and afraid. So soon, Father? So soon? I was doing well! We were all so hopeful and so grateful. Was that folly? Is it over now, with this wild joy of movement? Is this heart so grateful to beat that it will dance me to death? She was struggling to breathe evenly. She clenched her teeth. Not yet! It can't be time yet! Moisture sprang up on her forehead, on the palms of her hands, as she fluttered a hand helplessly at Dan. From far away she heard a male voice recounting blessings, bearing a testimony. It seemed she listened from another, far-off room.

"I think I'll be okay. Just let me catch my breath," she whispered hoarsely. Lenora felt as if she were running, running to catch her laughing, leaping breath as it loped ahead of her, always out of reach. Lenora tried to concentrate as she pushed away the fears that gnawed at her. She struggled and sweated at the mercy of her fluttering heart, until at last it tired of its exulting and slowed a little. Then a little more.

That had been happening often lately. She had taken the steroids to help prevent rejection of the transplanted organ. She had persevered as her voice grew deeper, her neck wider, her facial hair coarse, and her looks more masculine. Her once pretty face had become swollen and puffy. It was worth it, though, she thought, for another chance at life. To see Patsy reach junior high, to see Dallin ordained a teacher, and Jade reach Merrie Miss. And when those milestones came and went, Lenora set new goals to live for. She wanted to see her younger daughter receive her Young Women award for Beehives. She wanted to see her older daughter's team win the volleyball tournament next month and to watch as Dallin started high school. She didn't ask for much, she asserted, just the pleasures that any other mother would take for granted and dismiss, unimportant details in a crowded life.

And she wanted to talk to people, people like Reg, who didn't know there was anything else but here and now. They need me, too! she cried inwardly. I'm not finished yet! A sudden realization stung her. Maybe she would teach Reg again soon. Her heart leapt at the thought, as if anxious for the opportunity, and she labored to breathe evenly.

Oh, but her heart was so excited now! It had never in its other life known such love and gratitude. Perhaps it was too much for one muscle to bear, Lenora speculated. Perhaps it knew that its time was really up, and they had tricked it into living and beating and pushing her blood into her arms and legs and head and hands.

Dan held her close to him. She continued to cry quietly into his suit. He loved her so! How could she leave him? They spoke of it often, about her waiting for him in the next world. But Lenora had counseled the newly bereaved. She knew that Dan would be angry and very lonely when she died.

Lenora pulled a tissue from her pocket and wiped at her eyes. She gazed at the cheerfully patterned fabric of her dress and smiled. The outfit had been Dan's idea. She had dressed yesterday morning and was heading for the stairs to go down for breakfast. Moving quickly, he forced his square body between her and the staircase. Mischief glinted in his eyes. "You always wear such dark colors!" he groaned. "We are going shopping, and I am not going to bring you home until you buy something pretty and bright and happy to wear. Do you hear me, young lady?" She had laughed at his tone, as if he were talking to Patsy or Jade. With his brawny hand in hers, she hurried down the stairs and grabbed her old brown car coat.

They were like kids, Lenora recalled, strolling through the mall, holding hands and laughing at private jokes. They would not say it out loud, but they were building memories, filing glances and conversations away in their minds to be savored on other days. Dan sat patiently by three-way mirrors waiting for his wife to emerge, his broad face relaxed, wide gray eyes fixed upon the fitting room curtains. She tried on clothes in at least six stores until she saw Dan's broad grin as she left the changing room.

Her choice (well, Dan's really, she acknowledged) was a dress of swirling paisleys in bright pinks and turquoise. It had broad padded shoulders and big pockets. The wide pink belt made the outfit complete. Dan had selected turquoise earrings that shone against her hair, once black, now liberally flecked with white. Dan had been right. She felt fabulous and vibrant and alive as she wore it home. She felt strong. This morning as she put it on, she almost believed the fatal games her heart had been playing were over now. Her heart would be fine, she told herself: she would live to be ninety.

In the bathroom, as she applied her blush, it had happened again. Her heart had once more rejoiced too grandly, leaving her grasping at the sink, doubled in wonder at the wildness of it, waiting for it to slow down, afraid that it just might stop altogether.

She was suddenly faced with the knowledge that this could well be her final fast and testimony meeting. Lenora hugged herself tightly. Maybe this *was* the beginning of the end. Stunned, she looked around her at the toothbrushes littering the counter, the girls' hairbrushes, Dan's razor in a puddle of water—evidence of life in the busy home.

Fear and sorrow welled up inside her, and she sank to her knees on the cold bathroom floor. She prayed sincerely and hopefully to her Father in Heaven. He had seen her through so much already. He would not let her down. She asked humbly for strength to endure to the end. The end. When would that be?

She must not fall apart, she told herself, for the sake of the family. Please Father, let me have the faith to see this through with dignity and grace. Let me leave no loose ends, no hurt feelings or undue suffering. She must bring herself to accept the inevitable, she knew. Lenora whispered softly, "Thy will be done." She remembered her words to Reg: You won't hurt any more . . . It's peaceful . . . serene.

Lenora rose slowly from the bathroom floor and smoothed the skirt of her new dress. She looked in the mirror at her red eyes and shook her head. She must not go to church looking like this. It would make her grief too public. They will all know soon enough, if this is really it, she sighed. She ran cold water to splash on her swollen eyes and began to prepare herself.

She took extra care with her makeup. As she slowly and deliberately applied the eye shadow, the concealer over the dark circles, the lipstick and mascara and eyeliner, Lenora planned. She knew that on this day she must bear her testimony. It might be her last time, here. The ward must know that if she went, she went accepting God's design. She reviewed the words in her head. She would not express her fear that her time had come to leave them. But she must tell them . . . tell them that she was so grateful for life. And family and church . . . the exciting feeling—long past but never forgotten—of a baby leaping, growing inside. And the smell of rain. And muddy boots by the back door and wind howling outside while she made cookies with the kids. Camping trips when the children were little. And Daniel. She had told him so often, but she would tell him again, with the whole ward listening, how much she loved him. They would have all eternity together. Still, you wanted to say good-bye before the train pulled out, she thought ruefully.

She had notebooks, albums, videotapes, even birthday gifts squirreled away for her children's future. She would not leave them without her love; that was eternal. That would never die. Dallin and Patsy and Jade would someday leave this earth knowing their mother was watching, waiting to hold them in her arms again.

When they reunited she would stroke their heads and hold them close. She would say, "My, how you've grown!" They always hated it when people said that. They'd have a good laugh together over that one. It would be like when Dallin came home from Scout camp. Nothing dramatic, just hugging and talking and catching up on things. They would be in her mother-arms again, she knew, and she would do everything she could to keep the memories alive until then.

Lenora willed herself to breathe deeply and sit up straight, ignoring the fluttering that plagued her still. There was still the rest of the meeting, still a Primary class to teach. She would be fine, she commanded herself. She would be fine.

She decided she would ask Dan for another blessing when they got home. Right after she put the potatoes on to boil. The oil would flow, and his hands would rest warmly upon her head. She would be comforted. The stars and the rain and the flowers went on forever. She would too, she told herself. Her peaceful heart beat steadily, rhythmically, once more.

ANDREA:
THE PICTURE-PEOPLE SPEAK

Andrea was uncomfortable with these public displays of emotion that Mormons seemed to be so fond of. She thought of it as cheerleading for God. When Andrea was growing up, it was not fashionable to be religious, and if you were, you had the good sense to be quiet about it, for heaven's sake.

She sighed, exasperated. She was glad she didn't have to bear a testimony. She was not good at all this emoting stuff. At least Louise Sullivan hadn't fallen to pieces . . . not yet anyway, Andrea thought as she half-listened to Sister Sullivan.

Andrea's thoughts were diverted by her daughter; solemn, dark-eyed Tara passed her a folded piece of paper, looking hopefully into her mother's face.

If this was another one of her notes . . . ! But no, this time it was a picture. A girl with long brown hair, dressed in white, standing with a yellow-haired, mustached man, also in white. They were surrounded by a circle of blue water. Farther out, there was another circle, one of people. Smiling people. Big ones and little ones. It was a picture of a baptism.

Andrea ignored her daughter's questioning gaze. She knew Tara wanted an answer. Tara would have to wait. Andrea shifted in her seat, remembering the testimony of Virginia Thorne.

To Andrea, Virginia seemed to exemplify Mormon womanhood. She was fussily dressed, always calm and smiling, always graceful and in control. Her daughters were spotless and dressed as carefully as their mother. Andrea disliked Virginia, on the grounds that Virginia was everything Andrea had never been. Pampered, perfect, precious, Andrea thought bitterly.

Andrea had married a Mormon, the second marriage for both of them, and they were determined to blend their families as much as possible. She was willing to compromise because it meant so much to Derek. But at heart she was so different from these people, especially the women!

She crossed her legs and smoothed out the picture before her. Andrea looked for her face among those attending the baptism. Was that her? She did have a purple dress. Surely Tara would not have left her out?

She glanced sidelong at her daughters. Nine-year-old Tara was drawing again, her question unanswered. Little Amy, by her side, intently created her own masterpiece.

Amy drew a long cigar shape. A dog. It had six or seven legs and a very long tail. The dog stood under a large yellow ball, contemplating something orange that might be a flower.

Tara's pioneer girl was pushing a handcart. She wore a dress of corn-yellow calico and had long braids under the blue and red bonnet that she was filling in so carefully.

That was an image that was becoming part of Tara's legacy, Andrea admitted to herself. Although not born with Mormon pioneer ancestors, Tara listened raptly to stories of crickets and seagulls, of the hardships at Winter Quarters. And she loved to hear stories of her stepfather's ancestors setting out for Cardston, staunch members beginning an outpost of Zion.

And what was Tara's true heritage? Andrea asked herself. A beach bum father and a cynical mother.

Andrea had not been prepared for the harsh truths of single parenting. She had struggled to upgrade her education and become a surgical nurse, fighting as much for her daughters as for herself. Each day, as she had wrestled them all onto the bus, dragging the stroller and the diaper bag, clutching Amy with Tara hanging on to her sweater, she was keenly aware of her vulnerability. Every night she would look down at the curling linoleum floor of the kitchen, hearing the neighbors below, and become filled with resolve. Her girls' future would not be left to chance. And then she would haul out the textbooks and study veins and viscera until her eyes burned.

Amy had been a new baby then, blithely unaware of the struggle going on around her. Tara, however, had felt the full force of her father's absence and become almost a miniature adult. Andrea looked forward to the bus ride home from the day care center, when Tara would give a thorough account of her day and her sister's. No detail of Amy's care escaped her sister's scrutiny. Tara was Andrea's advocate and messenger, the oldest four-year-old in the country.

Moving to Canada from the humid warmth of Florida had been another jolting change for Tara. The excitement of fluffy white snow had deepened into the reality of frozen faces and a cold school bus every morning.

Andrea noted that Tara was trying very hard to adjust to her new family. She had gone out of her way to be agreeable to Derek's daughter and two sons. She had even given Julianne, her new sister, one of her most treasured sweatshirts. It was painfully evident to Andrea that her daughter wanted permanence.

And now she is asking to be baptized, Andrea thought, staring at the drawing she held. Why should I be surprised? She's been coming here now for six months, and all her friends in Primary are baptized. Every piece of paper she brings home from church reinforces it. Andrea pondered as she eyed the smiling, roundheaded girl in the drawing. The girl cheerily awaited Andrea's decision.

Tara was hungry for the embracing structure the Church offered. To her it was Family, a strong presence that promised never to leave. And Derek was the physical proof of that promise.

Andrea envied Derek his sureness, his "testimony," as they called it. It had been Derek's confidence that had first attracted her, so different from Steve's drifting ways. It had been a relief to find strength in someone besides herself.

Derek had often told Andrea how much the ward had helped him through the painful months of his divorce. Andrea remembered with a pang her own loneliness. She had cried at night many, many times, with no one but the moon to supplicate, to rage at.

Derek will always be there when I need him. And when the girls need him, she realized. And she had to admit that she did admire others in this ward, too. They certainly got things done.

"But," Andrea told her husband, "they're a bunch of Ward and June Cleavers. Happy families, happy incomes, happy houses."

Andrea was a survivor. She wanted her daughters to be survivors, too. Not just part of a crowd following the leader.

Tara was showing her pioneer girl to a friend behind her. Andrea remained deep in thought. The girl in the baptism picture had dark brown hair falling down her shoulders in two lumpy masses. She had pink lips stretched in an impossibly large grin across her face. Her eyelashes stuck up, four spikes over each brown eye. The man holding her, similarly roundheaded, wore the same smile, save only for the mustache above it.

Andrea smiled faintly. Tara loved Derek's tickly mustache. The drawing-Derek had an arm poised in the air beside him, ready to do the deed. Waiting for a signal. Then that grinning child would disappear under those blue felt-penned waters and perhaps come up a different person. Andrea wondered if she would come up with the same enormous pink smile.

"Oh, Tara!" she wanted to say, "this church doesn't just want you to show up on Sunday and chip into the collection plate. This church wants your *life!*"

Life was hectic already just looking after a family and holding down a job without looking after other people, too, Andrea thought, thank you very much. Tara was so serious. If she got baptized, Andrea believed she would become a Dutiful Daughter to the patriarchy of the Church.

Andrea imagined an aproned Tara endlessly baking and sewing and taking care of everyone's needs but her own. A perfect shell of a woman, empty inside. Which was precisely the way she pictured Virginia Thorne.

Is that really it? the picture-people wheedled. Or are you just jealous? Do you think we'll take her away from you? They smiled kindly up at her in their concern.

The child in the picture waited. She seemed to stand on tiptoe, caught in the moment before submersion.

Andrea folded the paper in half. She did enjoy coming here. She liked the "my brother went to Ricks with your missionary companion" familiarity these people had with one another. They seemed to try to draw her into their circle, pulling back when they sensed her reserve.

She knew she could attend every Sunday but never join. She couldn't swallow the doctrine whole, as Derek had. But then he'd been raised with it. It came naturally to him.

Tara was watching her again. Andrea did not turn to look. She knew there would be the unspoken question in Tara's dark eyes once more. She had promised to tell her today.

Andrea thought of the things she wanted for Tara. She wanted Tara to feel secure, to remain close to her, to have the kind of relationship Andrea had never had with her own parents. But Tara must be strong. If Tara got baptized, it would change her future in a very real way. She will grow away from me, Andrea said to herself. She will be part of them. She will lose the part of me I want to give her—strength to think for herself—and be swallowed up by this subculture. She yearns to be part of something so much.

Tara had drawn a ring of people standing behind the font. Andrea studied her carefully drawn details. The men all wore ties, and the women long, full dresses—Tara's idea of sophistication. The group stood silently, smiling, waiting patiently.

"Soon." They seemed to whisper sidelong to one another. "Just keep smiling. Soon she'll say yes." The stalwarts stood shoulder to shoulder by the water.

Andrea sighed. She had to tell her daughter today. She had put it off for weeks. The drawing was Tara's gentle reminder.

"I don't want to lose you, Baby," fell involuntarily, inaudibly, from Andrea's mouth.

Yesterday as she had set about the unhappy task of combing the tangles out of Tara's wet, shoulder-length hair, Tara had been strangely quiet. "Sister Bertram said when she got baptized, her hair floated on top of the water, and she had to get dunked again." Tara smiled and then added, "I bet that was pretty funny." She suddenly became sober. "Do you think mine would do that? Float, I mean." Tara stared at herself in the mirror above the new dresser. "I think I'd like to just go under once. Maybe you could braid it."

Andrea wondered how to answer. She concentrated on parting the brown strands evenly as she considered her reply. "I think you had better wait a while before you get baptized," she said at last. "I want you to be sure you know what you're doing. It's a big step. It would change your whole life, Tara Bear. It's a lot more than a quick dunk and a new dress and a party. It's your whole future. I . . . I'm not sure I want you to jump into anything."

"You don't jump in, Mom. You walk in. You can keep your eyes open if you want. Julianne says so."

"I didn't mean the actual water, Tara."

Her daughter's reflection gazed solemnly at her. "Neither did I," she said quietly. Andrea studied the pattern on the bedspread. This child is too old for her age, she thought sadly.

Tara took a deep breath. "Mom, I'm old enough to decide for myself. Sister Bertram says I have *agency*. I know the difference between right and wrong." Tara sighed and looked up at her mother, saying quietly, "It's wrong to be mean."

Andrea began combing again, tugging a little at the snarls in her daughter's hair. Her hand shook slightly. "Is that what you think?" Her voice rose a notch. "That I'm just being mean?" In reply, Tara studied the bow on her flannel nightgown. Her answer was slow and soft. "Maybe you just don't know any better."

This knot was beyond gentle coaxing. Andrea jerked the comb angrily. She felt a wrench of regret as Tara's eyes reddened with tears. Frustrated, Andrea threw the comb onto the bed. "For crying out loud, Tara! Don't push me!" The dark eyes flashed as tears brimmed and then fell. Tara ran to her own room.

Andrea's hands flew into the air angrily. Striding from the room, she avoided her face in the mirror. She paused at the doorway, gaining control, and then stepped softly across the hall to Tara's room. Tara lay sobbing, her face screened by a wet, dark curtain of hair. Andrea felt her throat tighten painfully. "I'm sorry, sweetheart," she murmured as she reached for her. Andrea sat down beside the huddled girl. She hugged Tara tightly, her hand cupping the damp warmth of her head. "Just a few more days, okay? I . . . I have to think about it some more."

She tried to rock Tara, but Tara would not be rocked. Andrea stroked her daughter's head gently. The girl burrowed into her mother's sweater, shaken but still unwilling to abandon her cause. "Tomorrow, Mom?" came the muffled plea.

Her voice was eager as she raised her eyes to her mother's. "Tell me tomorrow, so I can tell Sister Bertram in Primary!" Her eyes shone with tears and hope. Andrea smiled and wadded folds of pink blanket into her fist, squeezing tightly. She hesitated.

"All right, then. Tomorrow. Now brush your teeth." Andrea wiped Tara's flushed cheeks and looked into her daughter's face once more. Tara's eyes were dark and wide. So innocent. So trusting. Did Lenora Bertram have any idea how much her enthusiasm as a Primary teacher was keeping the two of them up at night?

As if summoned by Andrea's thoughts, Lenora Bertram stood up purposefully in the fast and testimony meeting and reached out a hand for a microphone. Andrea felt Derek's arm around her and looked into his hazel eyes. As he squeezed her, she sighed heavily.

What trials would Tara and then Amy have to face in the

years ahead? Support, Andrea admitted to herself, is hard to come by. She refolded the drawing and leaned forward, pressing it to her forehead.

Through the folded paper, the picture-people seemed to grin even more warmly, encouraged by her lack of resolve.

Andrea glanced at the clock, at the chorister, at the bishop and counselors on the stand. She looked at the people around her. These were the people her daughter wanted to join. She nervously rapped the folded paper against her leg as Sister Bertram cleared her throat and prepared to speak. Andrea unfolded the picture and fanned herself, ignoring the persistent stare of the picture-people.

The meeting was half over. She would have to make up her mind. Andrea smoothed the picture on her lap and tried to identify her daughter's Primary teacher among the depicted, ever hopeful Saints.

Sister Bertram's voice drew Andrea's gaze upward. Although the words trembled as they tumbled out, there was no hesitation, no apology in the fierce happiness they asserted. It seemed to Andrea that Sister Bertram had a light in her moonlike face that glowed brighter and brighter as she spoke. She poured unabashed feeling into her testimony, yet it seemed she was so direct, so determined to say it clearly. No wonder Tara was impressed by her Primary teacher.

Tara sat motionless, enthralled at her teacher's words. Words of death, words of life.

Sister Bertram spoke of the need to believe. She knew that the only reason she had come this far was that Heavenly Father had sustained her all those dark hours in the hospital. And many Saints had brought food, taken her children, said prayers. They had been there for her.

She'd had a heart transplant! Andrea had never known. How did her family stand the strain? They must always be wondering when the time would come, fearing it would come any week, any day now.

Andrea had seen a lot of transplant patients. Most didn't make it even five years. Lenora Bertram must know what her chances were. Yet she could stand here and be happy. Andrea recognized something of herself in Lenora's steely determination. Now here was a survivor.

Yes! the picture-people exclaimed through their fixed smiles. Yes!

The hair on Andrea's arms prickled. She felt Tara's deep gaze once more. The picture-people waited, everlastingly patient, tirelessly optimistic as the hands of the clock moved silently.

Andrea folded the paper quickly and moved to put it into her purse. Suddenly hesitating, she held it, fat and creased, in midair before her. She sighed and unfolded her daughter's carefully colored hopes. Then she smoothed the drawing once more on her lap. Lenora Bertram's face seemed to smile up from the paper, even as her words filled Andrea's ears. She was a strong woman. Andrea's gaze again strayed to her eldest daughter.

Tara's eyes were closed. In prayer? Andrea wondered, softening. She looked at the drawing in her lap. The picture-people smiled up at her happily. Tara would have her answer today.

RIKO: PRAIRIE LILY

Riko was having a difficult time concentrating on the testimonies borne before her. Her hands had stopped shaking, but her pulse was still fast. It had been an hour since her presidency had been approved, but Riko experienced it anew several times that morning: the knee-shaking, heart-thumping suspense as she awaited the ward's sustaining vote.

From up on the stand, Riko was allowed a glimpse of the ward that many members never see. A chorus of movement continually echoed about the chapel, increasing when the day was hot or the speaker long-winded. Imagining themselves to be just one of the crowd, many members were unguarded in their facial expressions as they faced the front. Riko saw one sister's forehead furrowed with concern as she stared into space. Another woman yawned hugely. One looked irritable and impatient, while behind that sister, a woman smiled contentedly as she kissed the top of a child's head. Riko had often thought it was as if she had a magic glass in front of her, enabling her to look into people's lives unnoticed.

She recalled once more how she had stood before them—a smile frozen on her face, her heart pounding furiously, waiting for their judgment. Her counselors and secretary were on their feet as well, but at least they had the consolation of not being up on the stand, sticking up like a rusty nail from an old board.

Riko had quickly glanced about. Most people seemed to accept the callings easily. Louise smiled up at her. "At last I can talk to her about this calling!" Riko thought with relief. Louise's face was suffused with delight and congratulations.

But there had been two or three sisters whose reactions were less enthusiastic. Riko watched as astonishment, disbelief, and acceptance chased each other across their faces.

After their initial hesitation, arms were raised to the square and faces were composed once more. Everyone managed to look as if Riko had been an obvious choice, as if it had been widely suspected for some time now. They craned their necks to look around the chapel for Riko's counselors and secretary.

Rhonda Fitzpatrick, her first counselor, had stood up near the front, looking as gracious as ever. She wore a classic suit, her shoulders back, hands clasped before her, her wide, beautiful mouth smiling warmly. I am so lucky to have a counselor like her! Riko had marveled. I wonder why they didn't ask her to be president instead of me? Rhonda is the kind of person who always knows just what to say and do . . . Of course, her husband's out of the picture, but at least she's had children. Riko looked forward to knowing Rhonda better. She had heard many examples of Rhonda's spiritual strength and her poise.

Sharon Rasmussen, Riko's second counselor, was way at the back, to Riko's left. She was average looking in appearance and height, except for the gorgeous russet hair that tumbled about her pale face. She was dressed in a blouse and a long, simple skirt over tan boots, topped with her usual soft woolen shawl. Riko had been surprised by her visit to Sharon's house. It was as if this sister hid herself from public view, reserving her creativity and charm for her comfortable home. In Riko's view, Sharon was a light that needed to come out from under her husband's bushel.

Riko did know that Sharon's husband would be out of town a lot. That was one reason Sharon had been somewhat reluctant to accept. That, and, as she herself falteringly put it, "I'm not really a people person . . . " her voice trailed off. Sharon pulled her cardigan around herself tighter, as if she could retreat into its bulky depths.

Riko had noticed that as Sharon stood before the ward today, she'd had her shawl wrapped snugly about her. She looked for all the world as if she wanted to pull it right over her head. Sharon fidgeted with a long red curl, her round face pinched slightly, and bit her lip as ward members looked her over. Riko reflected that Sharon could use some of Rhonda's confidence too. But from Riko's conversations with Sharon in the last few days, Riko had learned that Sharon radiated a special warmth to those she felt comfortable with.

And there was Virginia Thorne, not far from Rhonda, off to Riko's right. This woman is to be my secretary, thought Riko, with a faint touch of unease. Virginia looked to Riko like an over-blown rose, all ruffles and faux Victoriana in a fussy dress, her hair up in a crownlike braid. It was Riko's turn to bite her lip as she glanced at her secretary, who smiled under her heavy makeup. Riko reminded herself that faith is believing in things not seen. Virginia's careful attention to details might well prove valuable, she realized. After all, she had known that Virginia was the right one to choose; she had prayed about it and spoken with Bishop Malmgren. The incoming presidency now needed only the approval of the ward.

Riko held her breath at the bishop's words, "Any opposed, by the same sign?"

Not one hand came up, except for Sean Klassen's. Sean was only five. From up on the stand, Riko had witnessed Sean's cheerful opposition to every name put before the ward. She smiled at him, and he waved.

Now, as Riko sat listening to the testimonies of ward members, she looked with some foreboding at the slim book in her lap. "RELIEF SOCIETY," it proclaimed in large white letters against the blue background. In smaller letters below was printed the word "Handbook." It laid out the mission and purpose of the Relief Society and the responsibilities of the presidency. Riko flipped through it randomly. Duties of Pianist, Duties of Visiting Teaching Supervisors, of Compassionate Service Board Member, of Ward Counselor Responsible for Education—everyone had specific duties, all stated in numbing detail.

Riko scanned the Duties of Ward Relief Society President once more, a lengthy description. Lots of meetings: with the bishop, ward council, welfare services—Riko smiled at the next phrase— the ward committee for single adults. The president had specific welfare-related and compassionate service duties, oversaw visiting teaching and gave particular attention to single women, according to the book. Everything Riko needed was there in print before her, explaining how she was going to fulfill her calling. It seemed to tell the new president everything she needed to know, except what Riko needed to know most: how would she fit in with these women? Riko cringed slightly as she reread the sentence, "Represent the needs and viewpoints of the women of the ward."

Virginia had stood before the ward, porcelain perfect, and

borne her testimony. She'd spoken about her family, the blessings of her "wonderful" husband and her "sweet" daughters.

How can I represent her? Riko had asked herself, then as now. Riko wondered if she could even manage to find enough common ground with her counselors to work together fluently.

The handbook said that the Relief Society assists in fulfilling the threefold mission of the Church. Which, as any Merrie Miss can tell you, thought Riko, is (a) proclaim the gospel, (b) perfect the Saints, and (c) redeem the dead.

The problem with her being Relief Society president, thought Riko, was that (a) she didn't fit in, (b) she wasn't comfortable with some of the sisters, and (c) she hated working with a group. She would much rather make things happen on her own.

If only this job was as straightforward as her job at the Calgary *Herald*, Riko wished once more. Last night she had worked the five-to-midnight shift. She had no sooner crossed the buzzing newsroom to her workstation at the center than the weekend editor hurried over. "Riko!" Gary called, clearly upset. "I'm glad you're here. Listen, there's a bit of a problem with the front page of the Pulse section . . . " The Pulse section ran Sundays. It was a newsmagazine, a kaleidoscope of arts, lifestyles, and current affairs. Art for tomorrow's section should be well taken care of by now, Riko thought, surprised at the editor's words.

He motioned her over to his corner of the newsroom. "Look at this page." He called it up on the computer screen. Much of it was blank, the text framing a large hole where artwork should be. "Hal called in sick yesterday, and this was missed somehow. Color art for this story has to be done and off the composing room floor by ten o'clock." Gary's face was anxious. "How are you fixed for work tonight?"

Riko strode to her work area and reached for the hastily scrawled requests for illustrations piled on her assignment tray. She riffled through them, assessing. "Not bad tonight," she nodded. "I'll read through the story, and let it sit while I do this other stuff."

The editor's tense shoulders relaxed a bit. "Great, Riko. You're terrific. I owe you one."

Riko first scanned the Pulse story, the history of the famous Nutcracker ballet. "Unremarkable," she murmured upon finishing the piece. Better come up with something good to give it a lift.

Then, for the next hour and a half, she sat at her computer terminal, bathed in the colors that played across the screen before her. Riko was oblivious to the squawking of the police radio, the bantering of copy editors and the television that was never turned off. About her the room hummed and crackled with information and communication. Riko screened it out, focusing on the task at hand.

She tackled the demands of the assignment tray: the requests for graphs, charts, front page "boxcars," and other illustrations generated at the computer. Her eyes left the screen only to check her watch or the papers beside her as she plucked graphics from the wire service or created them on-screen. Instinctively, she selected the hues, the percentages of color saturation needed, the amount of gradation for "wash" backgrounds. These were mere technical details now, almost automatic to Riko. The challenge lay in making them look as good as they could and doing it quickly. Every time she pushed the key that would send a finished project to the electronic prepress department, she felt a quiet thrill of satisfaction.

Riko knew that she couldn't expect to create a masterpiece

every time. Usually her work was routine. Her creativity was nec-
essarily circumscribed by limited time and the utility of the project. As another artist at the *Herald* had put it, "at the end of the
day, it's all fish wrap." Not every piece could be exceptional.

But then there was the Nutcracker.

Every couple of weeks, Riko would be assigned what she
termed a "plum": a hand-done illustration, a chance to draw on
the full depth of her creative energies and let her imagination
soar. Then she would leave the unceasing chaos of the newsroom,
with its keyboards clacking, reporters on the phone, and the bab-
bling of radio and television sound bites. It took her only a minute to cross the noise-racked nerve center of the paper and enter
the first door on the right, the womblike silence of the lab.

Riko closed the lab door behind her, exhaling slowly. This
was her world. Here there were no police radios, no TVs, no tense
editors. The overhead lights were dim, and it was dark outside.
Through the large window, Riko could see the bright punctua-
tion of the city's downtown core. Nearby hung the airbrushing
board, colors swathed across its rough surface. Putty sculptures
were high on a shelf, seemingly animate vegetables for an upcom-
ing Food section. Little bottles of ink formed a haphazard circus
beside the sink, all bright colors and round shapes. There were
acrylic paints, chalk pastels, pencil crayons . . . Riko was surrounded by the tools and products of creation.

She sat down at her drafting table. A jointed wooden model
stood on the shelf beside her, a featureless person that she could
pose, casting it in whatever role she chose. It looked to Riko like
a mute and insensate Pinocchio. This faceless object she would
transform with pastels: on a cardboard sheet, it would become a
strong, graceful ballerina.

She worked steadily to light classical music, absorbed in her task. It was an oil pastel illustration—a scene from the ballet. Riko had been inspired by the paintings of Edgar Degas, but she heightened the impressionistic quality. Instead of filling in areas with a solid color, Riko splintered colors into their components. Light and shadow played together across the dancer, captured by the technique of single, separate strokes that worked together perfectly.

Periodically, Riko paused. She would narrow her eyes critically as she assessed her work and then go back to it with renewed vigor. Hours passed before she heard the door open. She glanced at her watch again. There was just time. "Come on in, Gary. I'm finishing up." She gave her work one last, satisfied look.

Gary glanced admiringly at the drawing. "Perfect. Absolutely perfect," he grinned at Riko. His eyes lingered on the picture as he left the room. "I'll get it downstairs!"

Riko smiled in acknowledgment of his words and left the lab for her workstation once more. She turned back to the graphs, the indexes, and the routine chores of her job. She could afford to relax a bit now. The night's deadlines had been met and mastered.

This morning she had not even bothered to throw a housecoat over her nightgown as she ran from her bedroom. Quickly unlocking and opening the front door, she ignored a blast of frigid air and reached out for her copy of the paper. It was cold to the touch and unfolded stiffly. Riko shut the door and crouched on the living room carpet. Quickly, she removed the top two sections of newspaper. There it was! The layout editor had set the headline in modified script, a deep royal blue. And her drawing had reproduced perfectly.

Each tiny stroke of pastel, a different color from its neighbor, had combined to meld into a seamless whole picture. That is the miracle of impressionism, Riko told herself again as she sat in sacrament meeting. That is why people seem to universally like it.

As she looked out at the ward members—their faces portraits of fatigue or joy, love or pain—she thought of them as strokes of color. Bright red, Ruth Boynton; bright pink, Lenora Bertram; yellows, blues, dull browns and blacks, white splashed here and there—all painted across the broad canvas of the chapel. Claude Monet, the impressionist, hadn't liked doing still lifes, she recalled. Yet his flower arrangements, captured with dots and dashes of paint, shimmered with light and were among his most transcendent creations. Lenora Bertram stood up. The people before Riko swayed and fluttered, the brushstrokes merged before Riko's eyes, and she saw the picture they formed. Flowers, stirring as if in a light breeze, turned toward the speaker. The image called forth a memory to Riko.

It was a hot day in late June, in Taber, the small town in southern Alberta where she had grown up. Riko was about nine or ten. She had run away from home. In her heavy heart she carried an unseen wound. In her arms she clutched a wrinkled paper grocery bag. It contained clothes, books, pencils, and crayons. Riko's mind was made up. She was going to live with her Grandma Ikuta. She would never go back. Her mother would be sorry.

Grandma, she knew, understood her. "For instance," the little girl muttered to no one as she hurried up Grandma's walk, "she doesn't call me Irene. She calls me my real name, Yuriko. Irene is the girl that Mother wants me to be. Yuriko is the girl that I am. Grandma loves me the way I am."

Grandma was coming down the white sidewalk, in a pair of navy stretch pants and an old striped golf shirt of Grandpa's. Her face smiled under her wide straw hat. Over her skinny arm she had a plastic bucket from her grandchildren's long-abandoned sandbox.

She did not ask Riko why she cried. "Put your bag on the step, Yuriko," she said quietly. "We will go and pick flowers for the *ikebana*." The *ikebana* was the careful floral arrangement Grandma made every week or so. The old woman headed down the sidewalk, her feet in their cheap tennis shoes taking her to the prairie.

She walked ahead of her granddaughter, shaded from the sun by her broad-brimmed hat, her small back bending to examine whatever caught her interest: rocks, grass, budding flowers. Riko followed, sniffling. She had run away from home, she explained to Grandma, and was going to live with her. Grandma did not speak, letting her story unwind itself as they walked.

"I was making such a beautiful drawing, Grandma! There was a girl who was riding a dragon, like the one you told me about. She was riding this dragon—he was her pet. And her hair was flying behind her like black clouds." Riko's hands grabbed her own heavy black hair and held it out behind her, in illustration. "And there was a little town below, and her family, and mountains. Remember we went to the mountains, Grandma?" Riko's grandmother nodded without turning around, her eyes searching the ground ahead of her. "I drew them way far away." Her thin arm pointed to the horizon. "Kind of purply blue, because that's how they looked to me . . . " Here she stopped and stamped her foot on the dry grass.

"And Mommy just threw it out. It wasn't garbage—it was perfect! The best drawing I've ever done! Ever." Riko stopped and looked defiantly at Grandma, who continued walking, bent like a stick, her pail over one arm. "She says drawing is stupid. She says," Riko mimicked her mother with wicked precision, "art doesn't buy groceries, Irene. Do your math immediately, and don't put it off one more second!" The girl's dark eyes filled with tears even as her brows drew together in anger. "I was going to do my rotten math. I just wasn't going to do it *yet*."

Yuriko waited for her grandmother to admit that she, Yuriko, was right and her mother wrong. She could see the side of Grandma's face, working as if to speak but not speaking. The girl, suddenly inspired, believed she knew the way to get Grandma Ikuta to take *her* side. Surely Grandma believed that Yuriko's mother, the former Arlene Jensen, would never understand the skill, the necessity, of seeing beauty.

Yuriko's voice rang out over the flat land between the two of them. "Grandma, is Mom right? Is drawing stupid?" Yuriko fervently believed that Grandma could not remain silent in the face of such blasphemy.

Amazingly, Grandma still did not reply. She did slow her step, allowing the girl to catch up to her, and reached out a wrinkled and spotted hand, taking the small, thin one in hers.

They walked together through the arid sunshine, past the white wooden fences of the town, the wide streets of Taber stretching before them, neatly dividing the rows of parched lawns under life-giving sprinklers. Everything looked the same as usual but different somehow. It seemed to the little girl that under her Grandma's all-seeing eyes, the landscape became sprinkled with tiny bright flecks of color.

As she walked in her grandmother's enchanted world, she was Yuriko. Irene was the name her friends called her, as they hollered out in kick-the-can or giggled over the phone. Irene was always getting heck from her mother. But now Irene was very far away, a strange girl Yuriko had known once, had dreamed of. Irene was magically transformed from a gum-chewing girl on the brink of blossoming into Yuriko, a watchful fairy-child who knew each wildflower as a friend.

Silently, Yuriko watched the thin slivers of water arc from the lawn sprinklers, flying high up into the air, and then splinter into crystal droplets onto the grass. "Ch! Ch! Ch! Chhhhhhhh!" The lawn sprinklers giggled and whispered, letting her in on their joke.

The prairie summer was still young, and Yuriko occasionally felt a cool breeze on her newly bared legs. She and Grandma did not stop as they reached the edge of town, venturing out onto the fields beyond.

Occasionally Yuriko would stoop and tuck a tiny wildflower in her hair. Into the blue pail Grandma gently placed fat round blossoms of sweet yellow clover, delicate purple harebells, tall buffalo beans with their bright drops of color. Grandma would find the small pointed faces of shooting stars, the delicate filigree of yarrow that smelled of earth and sky. And something else, something wonderful. Grandma had smiled and tickled her chin with it . . . yes. Riko slid deeper into the memory, closing her eyes.

She saw Grandma's dark eyes with their fretwork of wrinkles, heard her chirping voice. Yuriko felt the breeze stir the silky fronds of hair around her face as Grandma held her treasure to the sun. "Eh? What are you doing here all alone? So beautiful! Look, look, Yuriko! A lily!"

The prairie lily was the color of an overripe peach, a rich, luscious orange-yellow. Deep within, sprinkles of cinnamon dotted its throat and wide, curved petals. Its dark, cocoa-dusted stamens stretched to the sky, its stalk tall and strong. The girl gazed deeply into the voluptuous blossom, memorizing it to draw later, a silent rebellion.

The flat, cracked fields spread from their feet. Above them the sky stretched itself outward, upward, forever yearning. Grandma touched Yuriko lightly under the chin with the flower. "Strong. The lily is strong and beautiful," she smiled. "You are named for the lily: Yuriko." Grandma's eyes were brown as the richest earth. Silver and black hair waved gently about them. She looked down quickly, but not before Yuriko saw the moisture spring to her gaze in a sudden and quiet flood that ebbed as hast- ily as it had come. "You . . . you see with my eyes, my child. Beauty is everywhere, if you have eyes that see it. It is not . . . stupid." She spat the final word with distaste and then gently placed the lily's orange fire in her blue plastic pail. The thrill of rebellion grew bolder within Yuriko. She'd known it all along, she exulted. Grandma *didn't* agree with her mother; Grandma was on *her* side!

Back inside Grandma's cool house, Riko watched as Grandma arranged the flowers with minute care. They would go in her special spot, the alcove Grandma called a *tokonoma*. Riko recalled them, a tamed, trimmed profusion whose special grace Grandma alone had managed to see and show.

There was a carefully pruned gathering of the yellow buffalo beans above. That was *Shin*, Grandma explained. It represented heaven. Below was its complement, three small shooting stars pushing through yarrow lace. That was *Hakai*, earth.

Between *Shin* and *Hakai*, heaven and earth, was *Soe*. Grandma said that *Soe* was "a place of being." This was the place of honor in the arrangement, a symbol of one's role in the uni- verse. Between heaven and earth, as *Soe*, Grandma carefully placed the lily.

"You see, Yuriko," Grandma had said slowly, looking into her granddaughter's face, "everything has a place." She furrowed her forehead for a moment. "A place to belong, to create harmony."

And now Riko, sitting on the stand in a church, in the city, could feel herself the lily. She sat between heaven and earth, the blossoms all about her, Grandma's voice whispering.

"This lily is not like the other flowers," the papery voice spoke from Riko's awakened memory, "and that is its greatest blessing." Riko rose to bear her testimony.

RHONDA:
THE CLADDAGH RING

Rhonda Fitzpatrick's expression normally suggested a quiet sylvan pool. Serene and composed, her eyes seemed to hold hidden depths of understanding. She made it a point of pride to remain unruffled, whatever crisis might befall her. It was a policy that had served her well throughout her rocky marriage and her career.

Today, as Rhonda turned her gaze toward Riko Ikuta bearing her testimony on the stand, an astute observer would detect traces of agitation on the calm surface. There was a slightly deepened crease on the high pale forehead, and Rhonda's long fingers fidgeted with her rings. If only this calling were all I had to worry about! Rhonda thought in exasperation, in response to Riko's words from the stand.

Mick had come to her last night. Full of bluster and blarney as usual, but he had surprised her this time: he wanted a reconciliation.

"For heaven's sake!" She dismissed the possibility impatiently. They had been separated for nearly two years. If anything, they should be discussing a divorce, Rhonda thought with a twinge.

She told herself that Mick was just throwing his weight around again, trying to bend her to his will. But she hadn't quite convinced herself. Rhonda frowned slightly as she recalled his words.

Mick had a low, musical voice, with just a hint of brogue. His "gift of the gab" was legendary among their acquaintances, and he played it to the hilt. "Come on, darlin'. I'm here, hat in hand, on the doorstep of your heart. I'm beggin' now. Don't be hard, Rhonda. Let me in!" he had pleaded. He had managed to sound contrite and seductive at the same time. Well, she was not going to let the smooth words get the better of her. Not this time.

She had been a small-town girl when she met Mickey Fitzpatrick. He blew into Stavely like a warm chinook wind in a prairie cold snap. Big and Irish, he was charming ("as the very devil," her father said cynically) and handsome. He had come to work on a neighboring ranch, and within a week nearly every girl in town was hanging around the post office waiting to glimpse him as he picked up his mail. This fact did not escape Mick's notice. Back home he was a poor farm boy from County Monaghan. In Stavely he had an aura of being foreign, mysterious, and desirable. He knew a good thing when he saw it, and he did nothing to dispel any illusions.

Every girl in town knew that Mick stopped in at Myrtle's Cafe for pie and coffee at four o'clock. (He rarely had to pay for it, depending of course if Myrt herself waited on him, or one of her eligible waitresses.) Pretending he was oblivious to the commotion he left in his wake, Mick would sally from Myrtle's down to the post office. He would raise his hat and nod gallantly to Neva and Avis Heimbecker, who unfailingly awaited his arrival. The sisters would wave and giggle, their straps as far down on their shoulders as Stavely's passing matrons would permit. Mick sailed on good-humoredly, seemingly oblivious to the chirping and twittering of unmarried women that dogged his steps. The sound of birds teasing a cat.

Mickey Fitzpatrick had created quite a stir. But Rhonda told herself she was not interested in this brazen boor and the reckless pursuit he inspired. The man was just a man, after all.

She could not say exactly how she happened to be in the Stavely post office at four-thirty-one on that summer afternoon in 1966. She told herself it was coincidence, nothing more. Certainly it had nothing to do with his laughing eyes or cheerful banter.

"Hmm. Parcel to Cardston, eh?" She heard the unmistakable accent behind her. "That's where all the Mormons live!"

Rhonda felt a flush creeping up her neck. She refused to smile. She turned slowly to face him. The man was such a blowhard. A blowhard with nice eyes. They were the color of a clear August sky. "Well," Rhonda said as coolly as she could, "as I am a Mormon, and as I do not live in Cardston, I think we may conclude that not all Mormons live in Cardston." She inclined her head stiffly and turned away again, only the faintest hint of a smile at the corners of her mouth.

Mickey looked at the tight knot of hair over Rhonda's long neck, her straight back and squared shoulders. He never had been able to resist the lure of the unattainable. He began to whistle, watching the girl in front of him pretend to ignore him.

To the chagrin of the Heimbeckers and the waitresses and the other eligible females of Stavely, his attentions were now focused on the pursuit of one Rhonda Rodgers. She was considered by these scorned women as being a tall, plain girl with lank hair and a smart mouth. No boy in town or out of it had ever shown passing interest in her scant charms. It was a mystery to all but Mickey, who spoke glowingly of her dark mane of hair, her graceful figure, her quick wit. Everyone who heard Mickey recognized him as a smitten man.

Mick had to have her, and he courted her constantly. He worked on her icy reserve with his clownish humor and soft words. Her condescending retorts spurred him further. The man simply would not give up. Rhonda was always polite, sometimes genuinely touched, and often annoyed by Mick's open affection. She didn't know how to be courted, it had never happened to her before, and she was hesitant to open herself to ridicule or hurt. But her occasional wide smiles spurred Mick to greater heights of determination.

From their conversations, Rhonda believed Mickey to be self-serving and arrogant, in spite of his humor and obvious enjoyment of life. But then she overheard Willa Baines talking to Abby Spackman in Baines' Shoes. The two women were murmuring at the counter while Rhonda cleared her throat and stared at a loafer in her hand, wondering how long it would take Willa to get on over and measure her foot. As the two women talked in low tones, the name of Mickey Fitzpatrick caught Rhonda's attention. Slowly Rhonda put the shoe down and walked closer to the counter, pretending to study the wire rack of Kiwi shoe polish.

Willa Baines was talking. "Well, I don't care what Jack Pinegill said. That boy came in here with those little stairstep children of McReedy's, you know?" Willa's hand measured the children in the air before her, one-two-three. "And he bought them each a pair of Buster Browns. Not the cheap stuff. Said not to tell anyone, so I'm just telling you, mind. Those kids' feet had scabs on the toes, their old shoes were so small, and just falling apart . . . Can I help you, Rhonda?"

Rhonda hastily put down a jar of polish. "No, thanks. Wrong

shade," she blurted. The two older women exchanged a knowing look. Rhonda's cheeks grew hot as she hurried past Abby Spackman's bemused smile and out onto the sidewalk. That evening when Mickey came to call, Rhonda let him kiss her.

Later that night Mickey Fitzpatrick blew through the door of the hotel tavern. His face was flushed, and he was grinning. He slapped money down on the scarred surface of the bar. "A round for the house! I've made up my mind! I'm going to be a married man!" The patrons roared, the owner beamed, and the jukebox played until last call. The news became common knowledge within eighteen hours.

There was one problem with Mickey's announcement: he hadn't actually asked the bride-elect. Rhonda thought the first three phone calls to wish her well were pranksters. Imagine, her getting married! Who could have started such a rumor? But the calls kept coming, and the neighbors stopped in, and then Rhonda's beaming mother suggested going to Claresholm to look at dress patterns, in spite of Rhonda's protestations.

Stavely was abuzz with the amazing fact that a scrawny mud hen with a smart-aleck disposition should make such a "catch." Rhonda was at first dumbfounded and then very angry.

As for Mickey, he was contrite. "I'm sorry, my colleen," he said the next night. "I had made up my mind to ask you . . . "

"And it never occurred to you that I'd refuse? Do you think yourself that irresistible? I want a temple marriage, Mick. You can't give me that."

"Yes," he spoke quietly. "Yes I can, Rhonda. You'll see."

"I won't do it, Mick. I don't love you. And you don't love me."

"So you'll learn to love me. It can't be that hard." He smiled boyishly at her and put his arm around her waist. She pushed him away. "Rhonda, you want more than this, don't you?" He swept his hand around the Rodgerses' small, scrubbed kitchen with its faded wallpaper and chipped sink. "You want a home of your own, a family. Maybe in the city. I want a wife. A real wife, not a giggling, simpering schoolgirl. I want you." Mick reached down and took her hand, whispering, "I love you, Rhonda." He paused. "And you aren't going to get a better offer. I know you. You're the type that wants kids. Think about it." He kissed her tenderly on the cheek and then slammed out the screen door, whistling. "I'll call you tomorrow, sweetheart! We'll go get us a ring Monday!" he threw the words behind him as he sauntered across the side yard, his whistling finally fading into the dim streets.

Rhonda's eyes stung and her cheeks burned. "A better offer!" Rhonda clenched her fists. She knew she was plain; she had heard it all her life. She ran up to her room. In the mirror she glimpsed her red face and the wild straight hair now flying behind her. She flung herself on the old iron bedstead and heard it cry out in protest.

Rhonda lay sobbing for half an hour. Then she dried her eyes and climbed off the bed. She crossed the room and turned on the light. In front of the cheval mirror she smoothed her hair and coolly began to take stock.

Collarbone, wristbones, elbows, knees. She was all bones beneath the cotton print dress. Her hands and feet were large and wide.

Square shoulders. Straight back. Broad hips. ("Never mind, dear," her mother had said. "They're good for carrying babies." What babies? Rhonda wondered. Would she ever really have babies?)

Having unhappily surveyed her body, she shifted her gaze upward to her face.

Freckles. She sighed. Long nose. She continued the inventory.

Wide mouth. (A stubborn mouth, she told herself, determined not to spare her feelings.) Straight eyebrows.

Rhonda looked deeply into her reddened eyes, which she judged to be a mediocre hazel. "He's right," she murmured. "I am no catch." Rhonda told herself she wasn't likely to get another offer if she lived to be a hundred, and she knew it.

She crossed the room once more and flipped off the harsh overhead light. Staring out at patches of moonlight on the street below, she declared bitterly, "Well, that's that."

Mick was persistent in his desire to please Rhonda's father. Although Brother Rodgers had been wary, he was mollified by Mick's announcement that he would be baptized. He took the missionary discussions and demonstrated abject sincerity. Mickey Fitzpatrick wanted to marry their daughter, she had given her consent, and he was joining the Church. There was nothing left but to plan the wedding.

It had all happened so fast. Rhonda had vowed she would not marry until they could go to the temple, a year hence. The least Mick could do was wait, she thought. But that was not to be. Mick was anxious to move to Calgary; he'd had a job offer from a real estate company there. He persuaded everyone that the sooner he and Rhonda married and settled in the city, the sooner they could start a family, and the better it would be for all concerned. So Rhonda's girlhood dream had been compromised.

The years had been good to them in many ways. Mick did well enough at real estate to set up his own company. They went to the Alberta Temple together. They had two beautiful daughters, a spacious house on the park, and vacations in the sun. Rhonda had decorated the house tastefully and believed that she filled the role of Mother and Housekeeper perfectly.

It had proven much harder to fill the role of Wife. Rhonda found herself frequently biting back comments as she noticed flaws in her husband that had not been apparent during their hasty courtship. Rhonda rose early, as she deemed proper, and listened to the radio while bustling about doing chores. Mick put a pillow over his head and asked her to wake him at seven. Rhonda would sort the laundry by color and fabric, only to find that Mick had thrown a pair of grubby blue jeans in with a lace tablecloth once the machine had started. Rhonda was not impulsive. She liked to carefully prepare every detail when the Fitzpatricks entertained. On the other hand, Mick had an annoying habit of inviting people over on the spur of the moment. Or he would go golfing on a sunny Saturday and leave his wife with rosebushes to plant and a lawn to fertilize. And then there was the day the police had come to the door. They very politely had explained that Mick had neglected to pay several speeding tickets and had an outstanding fine of three hundred dollars. Every day became a stream of irritants, until Rhonda no longer held her annoyance in check. Her gentle reminders became exasperated demands.

And Mick was always touching her—putting on her coat, kissing her good-bye or hello or good morning or thank-you, his hand resting on her arm as he made a point or told a story. As if he owned me! Rhonda thought snappishly. She began to shrug away Mick's touch, pretending not to see the hurt in his eyes.

She ignored the rumors that surfaced from time to time about Mick's business. Perhaps deals went sour, and people might complain about being burned by Shamrock Realty, but nothing was ever proven. Rhonda felt it better not to involve herself with Mick's financial affairs. He had assured her that there were bonds in her name and that of course they were well insured.

And that was more of his big talk, reflected Rhonda.

Finally breaking under financial pressure at work and Rhonda's clear distaste for him at home, Mick had become miserable. He decided to leave. In the letter he left behind, he suggested that Rhonda marry again, for love this time. Marry again! And he had told her once that she would never find anyone else to take her! She would not give him the satisfaction, she sniffed. Let him pay alimony.

As Rhonda continued to read the letter, she made an awful discovery. Mick had driven his real estate business into the ground. He had taken loans and even put a second mortgage on the house. Desperate to increase profits, Mick had taken chances. In the end, his charm was not enough to convince the bankers he was still a worthwhile risk. He declared bankruptcy. Rhonda was on her own.

With no training and no experience working outside her home, she turned to the only career she could think of that might provide a living for herself and her daughters: real estate.

After the first few sales, her confidence soared. She dressed herself smartly, developing a tailored, classic style that suited her lean, graceful body. She held her breath and had the long, dark mane of hair cut to a short, sleek bob that flattered her high cheekbones and fashionably wide mouth. She treated herself to a manicure once a week and learned to pull together clothing in a way that few women master. Always a student of the scriptures, she was now a reference point in Relief Society and had taught Gospel Doctrine classes and seminary. Rhonda grew confident, and it showed. She became, in fact, a woman to be envied.

There was no room in her life for men, Rhonda asserted. Most of them seemed staid and bland, anyway. On the occasional evening when she had time to sit alone in front of the television, Rhonda wrapped a blanket about herself, holding herself within her own arms, and glanced about the tidy room. She told herself she was lucky to be shed of Mick. And she told herself that her priorities were her daughters, her job, and her church. She and the girls moved to a chic townhouse on the edge of a golf course. Now Colleen was studying at BYU and Fiona had just been married. By all accounts, she and the girls were doing well.

And last night Mickey had come blundering into this carefully constructed world and wreaked havoc.

Last night had been Fiona's wedding reception. It was held at home, among the tastefully framed prints and artistic lines of Rhonda's townhouse. She had noted Mick's arrival and then continued in her hostessing duties, strangely flustered. Mick looked awful, she thought, as if he had lost his best friend. And his eyes . . . His eyes had penetrated hers as soon as he'd walked in the door.

All evening, as she supervised caterers and introduced guests, Rhonda could feel Mick's sky blue gaze on her. Finally, she ushered the last guest but one out the door, and the tired newlyweds headed up the stairs. Rhonda wearily sank onto the pale rose sofa, her white hands on her forehead.

"Long day, my love?" Though he spoke quietly, Rhonda started at his words.

"Yes. It was lovely, wasn't it? Fiona looks so happy."

"She's got every reason to be. David seems like a fine boy. Good future." He paused. "And I suppose she loves him." Mick attempted a wry smile. It came out as a pained grimace.

"Yes," Rhonda said simply. "Yes, she loves him."

Mick studied a vase of freesias on the pale marble of the mantel. At last he spoke determinedly. "I made a muck of it, Rhonda. I wanted you to love me. I thought I could just . . . just take you and *make* you love me." His voice caught in his throat. "I was so unbelievably stupid!"

Mick paused, gaining control, and continued. "I wanted to make you happy." He sighed sorrowfully. "I loved your strength and your blasted muleheadedness. You didn't know that, did you?"

He began to pace on her gray and pink oriental carpet. "When I couldn't make it work, I was angry. I wanted to hurt you, make you see you needed me. But you didn't. I only drove you further from me. Further than I ever imagined you would go."

"You didn't believe I could beat you at your own game," Rhonda smiled tightly to conceal her agitation. She couldn't help but gloat a trifle as she said, "Poor old Mickey. Well, it's late. I'm off to bed." She rose and headed for the stairs.

"Rhonda." Mick spoke softly, his hand on her arm. "I want to talk with you. Please?" he added.

Rhonda studied his face. There was no trace of his former suavity. The confident demeanor that had made him so charismatic had vanished. He wore a pleading expression as he waited anxiously for her reply. She fought to keep her emotions in check. Why was she so shaken by him?

She sighed, "All right." Rhonda motioned to a chair. "But first I have to tell you, Mick, that I am very happy. I have earned this." She gestured about her, moving nervously from his touch. "I have a feeling I know what this is about. I am not going to take you back. You don't love me, and you never did. You want what you have always wanted. A housekeeper."

"That's not true!" Mick stared at her, aghast. Suddenly his handsome face crumbled and with it his controlled facade. "Oh, I wanted you to love me, but you wouldn't. You didn't ever really love me, and you held it up to me like a knife to my throat! I thought that you had feelings for me, but I was lying to myself. All bluster and no brains, as usual," he added bitterly.

The silence was punctuated by Mick's muffled sobs. The porcelain mantel clock measured the seconds carefully.

Rhonda hesitated. "No, Mick," she said gently. "That's not quite true. You weren't lying to yourself."

"Are you saying you were . . . you were . . . fond of me?"

She searched her heart for the answer. Her first impulse was to deny she had ever loved him and show him the door, but she knew she must be honest with herself, if not to him. She pushed her pride aside deliberately. Behind the games, the anger, and the careful sparring, was there love? The clock's hands moved jerkily. The ticking insisted: "Tell him, tell him, tell him."

"Yes," Rhonda said evasively, "I was fond of you at one time. But you didn't love me. You just wanted me."

"Rhonda, I've been a proud fool, but so have you! Rhonda, listen." Mick's blue eyes blazed through the tears as he spoke distinctly, "I loved you." Then, all pretense gone, he lifted his head and bellowed at the ceiling. "I still love you, Rhonda! I love you!" His flushed face shone and his eyes glistened. He looked for all the world like a sheepish teenager.

"You really . . . loved . . . me?" Rhonda stared helplessly. "All those years . . . you still loved me?"

"Loved you? Great heavens! Look at you, Rhonda. You're a strong, proud, beautiful woman. How could I not love you? I couldn't help it. I can't help it, Rhonda. I can't." He paused, ashamed. "I've missed you."

Rhonda looked up from the sofa.

"Now tell me, Rhonda. Did you ever . . . you know. Did you ever . . . feel love for me? Could you love me?" He clasped her hands eagerly.

Taken by surprise, she stared at the roses twining around each other on the carpet, until she could trust herself to speak without shaking. She raised her head and said slowly, "I did love you . . . once. When Colleen was born. Remember, you came into the room and brought me roses. I was so happy. We just stared and stared at her, at each other. We couldn't believe we had made this exquisite little person. We kept touching her hands . . . so delicate and fragile . . . " Rhonda's voice trailed off.

"Rhonda, say you forgive me! I'm begging you, on my knees." Indeed, he was on his knees on the wool carpet. He was so flamboyant, Rhonda thought, her anger rising again. "Come on, darlin'. I'm here, hat in hand, on the doorstep of your heart. I'm beggin' now. Don't be hard, Rhonda. Let me in! My poor heart is fair crackin' for want of you . . . " He was silenced by her gesture.

"Blarney." Rhonda tried to be curt, but she had to smile. "Always the blarney," she sighed.

Mick stood up. He would not accept defeat. His blue eyes looked deeply into her hazel green ones. "All right, Rhonda. No blarney. Just listen, okay?" She nodded. "Remember when I made that big kite for Fiona and Colleen?" His shining face brought the day back for Rhonda. The sky had been a blazing blue, the girls' hair had whipped about their faces in spite of their braids. They had all been laughing into the wind. The sound had been lost, carried upward in gusts that shook the kite, making it dance in the sky. Rhonda remembered what had happened next. "And then the crossbar snapped." Mick's face clouded. "We tried to make it work without it. But the kite would pitch and buck, and finally it would dive right to the ground, time after time after time." His hands sliced the air in front of him with emphasis. His voice became quiet. "I'm like that, Rhonda. A kite without a crossbar. No direction, no stability. No . . . you."

Mick paced for a few moments. "Look, let's be friends," he offered. "Truce. We'll see each other, go out to dinner once in a while. I'll try and be—more like you wanted me to be. Heck, you could love me again! Will you try?" He grinned self-consciously. "Remember how you always wanted to go to the Philharmonic? Look! Wednesday night!" He pulled two tickets from his wallet. "I swear, just friends." He held them out to her with his left hand, pleading, his eyes more terrible in their need than she had ever seen them. His hand shook. It still bore the *claddagh* ring she had given him on their wedding day. Two hands framing a heart. A crowned, golden heart. The *claddagh* . . . an Irish symbol of eternal friendship, eternal love. Hers had been hidden in a velvet box upstairs for two years.

Mick's face was suffused with hope.

It seemed to Rhonda that the weight of years hung on that moment. Any second now she would reply, and the course of her life might be changed once again.

"Well, maybe." Her reply stunned her momentarily. "I . . . I'll give you a call," she finished lamely.

Rhonda sighed as she automatically picked up a crayon tossed by the Klassen boy behind her. Glenda Klassen was vainly trying to prevail against the unstoppable tide of her children's energy. As she passed the crayon back, Rhonda stared at her hand, at the rings on her tapered fingers.

Could she have been happy with Mick? He loved her, and she had loved him, once. But he was so . . . well, he was Mick. Dramatic and impulsive and moody. She recalled his hand on her arm and then his warm grip on her hands. It had been so good to feel his touch again. It had been so long. She hadn't realized how she'd grown to miss it.

But what, Heavenly Father, what could she do now? Surely it was too late to start again?

Riko sat down on the stand. The meeting was nearing its end. The bishop stood once more and began to speak.

Rhonda Rodgers Fitzpatrick glanced down, twisting her rings. Outstretched hands framing a crowned, golden heart. The slight crease on her smooth forehead deepened.

GLENDA:
BUILDING TABERNACLES

Glenda Klassen clenched back a yawn. She felt her husband's gaze upon her as she struggled to free Jonathan's hand. He had twisted it in his suspenders again. She sighed and pushed damp hair from her forehead. Why couldn't he just wear them without playing with them?

Ordinarily she liked to look at her husband, Frank, as he sat up on the stand. He was a handsome man, tall, slightly balding. He had a relaxed way of speaking that invited the listener to be comfortable. His calm face exuded confidence. She guessed that was one reason he was such a good dentist and an asset to the bishop as his second counselor. But today she did not want to face him.

She pulled the little boys apart and sent Sean to sit with his older brother. She was careful to be preoccupied with the needs of the children, not to look at Frank. She had never been able to hide anything from him. Her body craved sleep as a parched throat craves water: incessantly, relentlessly.

The meeting was nearing its end, and the children were restless. Up on the stand, Frank motioned for Elly to come and sit with him. Big deal, thought Glenda. If he wants to help, he could take Jonathan or Sean. Those two were the most difficult of the seven. Elly was like her father, easygoing and placid. She tiptoed to the front and sat with her daddy. Glenda's stomach lurched threateningly. Five of the other six children continued to squirm. The older ones shushed the younger ones. The younger ones made faces at the older ones. Sean untied Patrick's shoelaces. Joanna was sneaking some of Corinna's lip gloss. Only the baby slept, oblivious to the flow of the family about her.

"No more babies," Frank had said, after Jonathan was born three years ago. "It is too hard on you, Glenda. It's too hard on us." With postpartum hormones still raging in her bloodstream, Glenda could only stroke Jonathan's curled fist and shake her head. Her eyes, overflowing, said what she could not. Filled with the sight of Jonathan's round hard head, the aura of birth and maternity still bright about her own tired body, Glenda could not, would not, agree to Frank's ultimatum.

She quit nursing the baby that summer. She was pregnant before Christmas.

She had never, before or since, seen her usually calm husband so furious. Well, she *had* thought it was a safe time. Anyone can make a mistake.

"How many, Glenda? When does it stop? We can't just keep having children until you grow old." Frank's face was tense and flushed. He ran his hands through his thinning brown hair and looked at her in desperation. His hazel eyes were wide with disbelief and anger. "We have to care for every one of them. Every new child means more years of work for both of us." His voice softened as he turned to her. "Especially for you. It wears you out, Glenda. You're so tired. These kids take up every second of your day. When was the last time you did anything for yourself? When was the last time we went anywhere, just the two of us? I'm telling you, Glenda, we need a life together again." Frank turned away from her and stared out the bedroom window at children throwing snowballs at each other.

She could only gaze sadly at his straight back and the hard muscles of his jawline, wishing he would just go back to the office and forget about this for a while. She pulled her feet up, curling into the big armchair. At last she spoke quietly, almost whispering. "This baby was meant to be, Frank. I know it. Heavenly Father will tell me when it's time to stop."

Frank threw his hands into the air. His voice rose again. "Maybe He *is* telling you, Glenda. Dr. Kennedy says it's getting too dangerous. We're so lucky all our kids are healthy!" Frank turned and moved to her side slowly. "You're thirty-nine next month, Glenda. You know the risks." He knelt to look into her heart-shaped face. "And it's getting harder for you to bounce back than it used to be . . . Honey, we have to concentrate on the ones we have! This is absolutely the last one, right?" His voice was gentle, coaxing.

Glenda hesitated. Outside, the sounds of children rose to their window. "Right," she whispered.

Frank sighed heavily as he encircled her in his arms. She knew he hated to argue. "Good girl." He kissed the top of her blonde curls. Glenda fervently hoped he did not see the threads of silver among them. "You've done your part, Sweetheart. This baby will be our grand finale."

And now here she was, Katrina Annette, our Katy Ann, our little Katybug, smiled Glenda as she gently untangled a barrette from Katy's wavy hair. She was a year and a half now, and she must have known that her father had had doubts about her before she was born, because she had worked her way into his heart so diligently that Frank hated to be away from her for any length of time.

As soon as Frank got in the door at night, he would find Katy Ann and scoop her up in a wild frenzy of tickling and laughing. If he ever forgot this important ritual, Katy would scream and howl with rage. Glenda had seen Frank literally drop his work at the door, leaving everything and everyone on hold just to get at his little girl.

Many times he had expressed his thankfulness that she had been born. Glenda had known he would. When Frank bore his testimony, he expressed gratitude for his seven children and his faithful and righteous wife. He laughed as he pointed out that now their family had grown so big, they had to be listed on two health insurance cards.

Glenda looked over her shoulder uneasily. She was certain the other members were noticing the buzz of activity in the Klassens' pew. Her glance reassured her. It seemed to her that she saw several other mothers all trying to hush their children, all glancing nervously around to see if they would be caught in their impatience, in their imperfection.

It was too warm in the chapel, Glenda thought. Far too warm. She dabbed at her forehead quickly, stealing a glance up at Frank as she did so.

Should she tell him? How could she after last night?

Frank had been putting his supper into the microwave. It was ten o'clock. Around them the house settled. The older children were all baby-sitting elsewhere or at friends' houses, the younger ones asleep. This was the peaceful reward time that helped Glenda pull herself through her long days. She stood at the kitchen table folding laundry and listening to an old Van Morrison album. This would be as good a time as any to tell Frank what preyed on her mind. They didn't often get time alone. Awkwardly, she tried to broach the subject.

"Katy Ann is sure growing up. She's really not a baby any more." Glenda kept her tone light, busily folding as she spoke. "This morning she went and got herself a new diaper when she wanted to be changed."

Frank sighed. "Thank goodness. It will be nice when she's out of diapers entirely. And to retire the crib. And to not find half-finished bottles of juice stuck between the sofa cushions." He smiled as he took his plate to the table and sat down facing his wife. "Can you imagine it, Glenda? A kitchen without a high chair?" He motioned to the well-used high chair in the corner, with its cracking vinyl seat. Glenda's eyes lingered on the pablum-encrusted crevices and the scratched plastic tray that wrapped itself around the chair.

"No," Glenda murmured, carefully folding a pair of tiny pink overalls. "I can't."

"Honey, I know you're feeling a bit lost . . . our last baby is getting big." Frank stood and walked around to Glenda. He put his arms around her and looked down into her eyes. "But think of the freedom! When Katy Ann goes to school in a few years, you'll have some time to yourself again. You could take some courses, do all the sewing you want, do some stuff for yourself." His big hand stroked her back. "And we'll take more family vacations. We won't have to truck all the baby stuff and worry about naps." Frank paused and took her chin in his hand. He lifted her face to his. She bit her lip. She should tell him, right now.

Frank hesitated and then added, "I miss you, Glenda. We're all so busy, and that's fine, but . . . you and I don't spend the time together that we need to. We'll have more time together, maybe even go away for some weekends . . . just us." He kissed her tenderly and then drew her closer to him. Glenda buried her face against the scratchy warmth of his neck, feeling the strength of his arms around her tired body. He rested his chin on her head and she felt her body relax against his. It seemed like ages since they had stood like this, holding each other and listening to music.

She couldn't tell him then that her period was nearly two weeks late. Maybe it would come tomorrow. Maybe she was making a big deal about nothing, after all.

As she tried to focus on Riko's testimony, a crashing wave of nausea hit Glenda suddenly and then as quickly receded. She'd had this with every single pregnancy. Oh, how am I going to tell him? she wailed inwardly.

She would tell him again that their children were her mission in life, her everything. She cried over every tacky handmade Mother's Day card and bookmark. She had boxes of faded construction paper creations laboriously made, each child's showing a different, emerging personality. And each child was her creation, laborious but fascinating in its development.

Yes, she was tired. Yes, she looked forward to the day when she could schedule a haircut without consulting her detailed appointment book and cross-checking it with the family calendar. It would be a treat to make a meal that everyone could and would eat, for instance, or to sleep in on Saturday morning and have everyone get their own breakfast. But it won't be like this forever, Glenda reminded herself often as she rose from prayers to crawl tiredly into bed.

There were rewards, too. Those nights when a child cried for help and only she could soothe the demons that raged in his room . . . the day when she found an unexpected and supposedly anonymous note with three kinds of weeds, carefully placed in the vase on the table . . . dancing in the kitchen with the babies in her arms and the teenagers laughing and shaking their heads . . . giggling with Corinna in the darkened living room at her account of the geeky guy she'd gone to the dance with . . . She drew strength from these things, from the very individuals that enervated and exhausted her.

Some days it seemed as if every minute of her time was spoken for, but she was a good organizer. With detailed lists and calendars for every child, they all somehow made it to piano and gymnastics and basketball and band and drama rehearsals. And the children did not lack for anything. In fact, it was Glenda's firm belief that the children were blessed to be born into such a family. Frank's practice supported them well. They had a gospel-oriented home. They cared for one another (usually). And they did household chores. The older kids knew how to do laundry and prepare meals. They were much more responsible than most children their age.

If she wanted to have babies, then why should anyone else care? How many times had she heard "It's my body, it's my life"? Well, if the feminists could use that argument, so could she.

"It's my body, and if I can live with nausea and stretch marks and bleeding and sleeplessness, it's my business." Except that reasoning left out an important part of the equation: Frank.

Glenda smiled as she accepted the crayon that Rhonda Fitzpatrick politely handed back to her. Rhonda looked put out. Glenda made a mental note not to sit behind her in the future. Perhaps Rhonda's new calling would soften her a bit, she thought hopefully.

Glenda gripped the back of the pew ahead and let her head drop onto her hand. She drew a deep breath, cursing all panty hose as she did so. She was sure Frank was looking at her and dared not raise her eyes to his. She breathed deeply, slowly, until she could once again sit up.

She studied the silk flowers on the pulpit, and the chorister's lovely green dress. She could not imagine how they could hold a sacrament meeting without Riko up there. But they would have to soon. An unusual choice for a president, Glenda thought, but after all, the bishopric knew what they were doing. It would be interesting to see how Riko handled the calling.

Glenda pretended to watch Riko speaking, trying to see her husband's face from the corner of her eye.

Yes, he was looking at her again. Surely he must suspect something?

She could hear the whispering and rustling of her restless children as the meeting drew to a close. Glenda permitted herself a glance at the clock. Not much longer. She gently pulled a crayon from three-year-old Jonathan's mouth. "No, honey. Ucky." It was a mystery to her why some children felt the need to eat crayons. She caught Corinna brushing her hair and gave her "the look." Her gaze skimmed her husband's face and continued to the chapel around her.

Ruth Boynton seemed lost in thought. What was worrying her so? Glenda made a mental note to ask the Relief Society president if everything was all right at the Boyntons'. Maybe I'll just run some muffins over, she thought. At the image of muffin batter, pale, sticky, and heavy, Glenda's stomach twinged forebodingly. She would have Corinna make them.

Sean seemed intent on making Joanna's life miserable. He had just licked his fingers and smeared them on Jo's glasses. Glenda noted Frank's disapproving glare.

There was Louise Sullivan with her little adopted boy. How sad! To have to adopt. And then to have only the one. Glenda wondered if Louise and Bryce were going to get another baby. She hoped so. With a start Glenda realized that she and Sharon Rasmussen had better get over and visit teach Louise this month. Christmas would be here before they knew it. Sharon might even give the message this month, Glenda thought. She was starting to open up to the sisters they visit taught.

Glenda allowed herself to look up at the front again. Frank looked tired. He has got to take a little holiday, she thought, realizing sadly that was impossible, for either of them. If anything, this month would be busier than ever, with the kids off school for Christmas break. Of course, they would all go to the cabin, she knew. But, as fun as they might be, vacations with the children were exhausting, and Glenda did not count them as real vacations.

Sensing her glance, Frank turned his eyes to her. He straightened in his seat and leaned forward intently. Glenda looked away. Her conscience pricked her. She had to tell him. Maybe he knew already? Surely it must have crossed his mind. What would he say?

What could he say? It was, as Patrick would put it, a done deal. She had been *fairly* certain that it was a safe time of the month. And Glenda just knew that somewhere, a little spirit was so excited to come to their home. If Dr. Kennedy had a problem with that, well, they would just have to get a new doctor.

Frank had been so open with her last night, so honest about his feelings. And she had not told him. There were sins of omission too, she reminded herself. She should have told him then.

Hymn number 152. The chorister rose as the organist began the introduction. Glenda reached for the hymnbook and stopped, her hand in midair. Her stomach lurched yet again. Her face felt very warm and was immediately chilled by the moisture that sprang to her forehead. The ominous agitation of nausea resumed, growing in threat. She knew she could not fight it down this time. She had to get to the rest room.

Glenda gently lifted Katy Ann's head from her lap and laid it beside her, swallowing hard. She clutched the back of the pew again, preparing to stand.

As she did so, her husband's eyes held hers at last. Glenda's face flushed. She was caught, unable to look away. Frank wore a worried, almost stern expression. Stricken, Glenda was certain he read the truth on her undefended face. Frank's eyes widened as Glenda smiled weakly, silently pleading. But concern for her husband was soon eclipsed by the churning within her. She could no longer put off the inevitable.

Glenda stood up, her face slack, unseeing eyes still upon Frank. She was unaware of anything except the need to leave, quickly. She dashed from the pew and, tossing a last anguished glance over her shoulder, walked as fast as she dared down the aisle. Katy Ann's startled wail rose behind her, an anguished prelude.

SHARON: IT'S NOT RICHARD

Everywhere Sharon Rasmussen looked, she saw happy couples. That only served to remind her of the empty chair at the kitchen table and the wooden tag that hung, unmoved, on the family home evening chart. Richard had been gone for two weeks. Just one more to go, Sharon had told herself. Just another week, and then he'll be here. And gone again.

Trying to distract herself from Richard's absence, Sharon looked about her. Far ahead sat old Sister Bird, dozing off again, Sharon noted. This close to the end of the meeting, Sister Bird almost always fell asleep. She must not care what people think. Maybe it just doesn't matter to her anymore, Sharon thought somewhat enviously. Sharon herself would love to feel that way sometimes, to drop her shyness like a useless cocoon and do whatever the heck she wanted. Still, she clung to it. It was a known and safe cocoon.

But no matter what, I would never fall asleep in church, Sharon vowed. Esther Bird had even been said to snore through the sacrament prayer, although not often, and always gently. Not me, Sharon was aghast. I would just die!

Sharon let her gaze move from the sparse tufts on Sister Bird's head. The Klassen children sat a few rows behind Sister Bird, a whole pew full of them. Glenda looked thoughtful; the children, obedient. How did Glenda get out the door on Sunday with all her kids looking so neat? Sharon wondered. She theorized that since Glenda had nearly twice as many children as she did, hers ought to look at least as presentable as Glenda's. The Klassen children looked like a time-lapse picture of Frank Klassen growing up, Sharon thought. All with his face, only different sizes. Sharon smiled thinly.

She looked for the couple whose child had been blessed earlier in the meeting. Louise and Bryce Sullivan beamed at one another. Bryce Sullivan's arm encircled his wife and son.

Sharon ached to feel a comforting arm around her own shoulders. The last week had been a hard one. This was one of those Sundays when getting to church was so difficult that staying home had almost seemed an option. She wondered why she always woke up tired these days, as if the day's enthusiasm had been stolen just after her eyelids fluttered open.

One more week to go. Seven more days. And, hardest of all, seven more nights. She would stay up too late, delaying the inevitable solitary trek up the stairs. It was best just to go to bed bone-tired and fall into a deep and dreamless sleep right away. It was best to keep her mind full of the children's activities and her hobbies, anything but Richard.

Richard. Last night she had made the mistake of climbing into bed while she still had her wits about her. She had thought she would lie there and think about her new calling. Instead, her whole body yearned for Richard's touch. Her head turned fitfully on the pillow, finding it a poor substitute for his shoulder. Sharon's arms, unbidden, hugged blankets close to her face. Richard! She finally threw the pillow at the wall. Just come home!

This morning when she'd awakened to the vacant space beside her in bed, she squeezed her eyes shut. She could pretend he was there, still asleep, she told herself. But it was no use. His side of the bed was cool to Sharon's fingertips. He was just not there.

Sharon then opened her eyes to the dim light. In one determined motion, she threw back the flowered duvet and rolled out of bed and onto her knees.

Her prayer finished, she remained on the floor. The air was cool to her toes, and nubs of carpet insisted themselves through her nightgown. She rested her head on her still warm side of the bed, reasoning, When you don't feel like going to church, that's when you get the most out of it, especially at fast and testimony meeting. She stood up slowly, leaning on the bed as she rose.

Sharon then slid into her slippers and pulled her housecoat from its tole-painted hook, shrugging it on. It was time to wake up Janie and Megan, her youngest daughters. They were both speaking in Primary this afternoon and they still needed to write their talks. She could handle this, she'd told her reflection above the antique dresser with its ruffled scarf. It was just another Sunday without Richard. She flipped on the hall light and turned up the furnace.

Sharon paused outside the little girls' bedroom. I *have* to be there today, she realized with a start. The sustaining! She shivered with dread and tied her robe about her. All those people looking at me!

Sharon bent over her daughter Megan's sleeping form, stroking

the thin shoulder gently. She wished she'd had time to pick up
the dry cleaning this week. What could she wear? She moved
from room to room, preoccupied, checking on ten-year-old
Andrew and the nearly teenaged Sarah, closing their doors gently.

And there had been the Primary talks, the waking of the
older children, the children's breakfast, the many baths, the little
girls' hair, Sarah's lost shoe, and Andrew's tie, and then the little
girls were hungry again . . . Somehow they had got it all
together, but still they had arrived at church a few minutes late.
They'd tiptoed in during the opening hymn and slid onto a bench
a few rows from the back. But, Sharon comforted herself, we're
here, anyway.

Richard would have made breakfast. He would have supervised the downstairs bathroom while she supervised the upstairs
one. He would have helped Andrew tie his tie. He would have
warmed up the car while Sharon put on her makeup. It was so
much easier when Richard was home, Sharon thought longingly.

They had both agreed that he should quit his job last spring.
He was unhappy with the way the law firm handled the clients, as
if they were faceless vats of money waiting to be siphoned.
Richard knew better. He knew there were individuals behind
those faces, people who often suffered. And Richard felt the firm
was trying to make him one of the team, one of them. That was
not Richard's way.

Richard was always in motion, always had a wry comment or
quick witticism, no matter what the situation. As Sharon stood
on the sidelines, watching Richard dart through their world, she
felt earthbound, heavy.

Sharon was often slow to speak, wanting to get the words just
right before they came out. While she hesitated, Richard's words
poured out of him in a sometimes fiery torrent. His words could

catch and hold the listener in their bright-pictured eloquence, his hands underlining them with decisive strokes.

Sharon was always uncomfortable at gatherings. She preferred her home. She loved to surround herself with her house; it seemed to her like a warm quilt between her and the harshness of the world.

She pulled her shawl about her once more, thinking of Richard's curiosity and enthusiasm. Richard helped her to find the part of her that loved all kinds of people, their stories and failings and strengths, their ideas.

He loved to play the devil's advocate to startle others. He enjoyed catching them off guard, making them defend the easily mouthed platitudes they rarely thought about. She would never have the nerve to do that, but then, she supposed that was what had attracted her to him in the first place: his confidence.

She and Richard had been certain that he would find another position or perhaps work as a consultant. The couple had read the employment section of the paper together and carefully worked out a budget. They could last six months, if they had to. And they had their food supply. They were optimistic as they faced the future, knowing it would hold good things for them, for they were good people.

It had been like a holiday for a while. The children were happy to have Richard around more often, and Sharon enjoyed his company. They really were best friends. Richard kept busy in his basement office, doing bits of work here and there, sending letters to contacts, keeping all the lines open. And four and a half months went by. They began to grow nervous. Christmas was two months away, with all its extra expenses. The food supply would hold out for another couple of months, but there would be mortgage payments and Andrew's braces. And there were basketball fees and birthday parties and new jeans . . . the minutiae of daily life that had not been worked into their careful budget. Richard spent a lot of time in his office reading his scriptures, wondering what on earth he would do to provide for his family. They prayed for a small miracle, just enough to see them through.

It was not quite as they had hoped, but they did get a practical, although temporary, solution. A former colleague of Richard's phoned him out of the blue and offered him a six-month job—with a catch: it was on almost the other side of the country, in Ottawa. So he was gone for three weeks and home for one.

In the time he was away from his family, Sharon knew, her husband threw himself into his work, avoiding his home away from home, a sterile bachelor suite complete with kitchenette and room service. Richard wrote long letters to his wife, telling her of the arid life he lived away from them and remembering things they had done together.

His last letter recalled the time he had tried to teach her to cross-country ski. "Remember? You fell in the snow. It flew all around you and you giggled and thrashed. You tried to throw snow at me and missed—as usual!" He had helped her up. He recounted how Sharon's hat of soft green wool was dusted in white. Flakes clung to her lashes and her long red curls. Her cheeks were pink with the cold, and she had kissed him, still giggling helplessly at her hopelessness.

She remembered. She'd teased him: "I do love you, Richard, but how on earth do you expect me to walk with boards on my feet! You're out of your mind!"

Richard's letter continued, "We spent that night in front of the fire, remember? I'll never forget it . . . "

They wrote each other often, sometimes twice a day. The

phone bill was at an all-time high as they tried to push their feelings and desires through tiny wires. They wanted so badly to tell each other everything, to feel each other's warmth.

Only five places at the table. An empty chair at family home evening. Sharon pictured the handsome wing chair she had upholstered with Richard in mind, the one in the corner by the bookshelf.

As if things had not been hard already, as if Sharon was undergoing some kind of cosmic test, Riko Ikuta had asked for her to be second counselor in the Relief Society presidency. Sharon's first impulse had been to refuse, feeling that she could not cope with one more demand. Riko changed that.

The two women had sat in the Rasmussen living room, enjoying the warmth of an evening fire. This was Sharon's favorite room in the house, and it showed. Every piece of furniture in it had been somehow shaped by her hand, carefully upholstered, or sanded and refinished, or draped lovingly with a crocheted cloth. A wooden plaque hung above the fireplace, holding several tole-painted teddy bears, each labeled with a family member's name. They hung under pegs labeled "Prayer," "Lesson," "Scripture," "Song," "Story," and "Refreshments." Along the curved top was painted the message "Beary Happy Family." There were carefully arranged bunches of baby's breath and dried roses, the children's school pictures, and a family portrait. Cushions, hand-sewn and embroidered, matched the valances Sharon had made.

Riko stared frankly around her. "This is beautiful!" she exclaimed. "It's so . . . homey and cozy. And so elegant at the same time. You have a real knack for decorating, Sharon. My place is like a barracks compared to this."

Riko seated herself on the chintz-covered love seat. Sharon, blushing, sat beside her. They made idle conversation for a few minutes. At last Riko leaned toward Sharon and spoke seriously. Her eyes looked even darker than usual in the firelight. "I know you've never done anything like this before, Sharon. Neither have I. But I have prayed about this a lot in the last few days." She smiled, "I was so happy to hear you'd be my second counselor!"

Sharon turned away and watched the fire for a few moments. "I think maybe this is—a mistake," she at last blurted out. "I just don't know if I can do this." She told Riko she'd never been comfortable in front of groups. It was hard for her to talk even one to one, as the two of them were doing that moment. "How will I ever be the wonderful, chatty, homemaking counselor that everyone expects?"

Riko took Sharon's hand. "I know," she said. "I know what you mean. I felt kind of the same way. But after I prayed about it, I realized that the calling is bigger than I am, or you are. We need to put our own problems aside."

"I am not very compassionate," Sharon pleaded. "Lots of times I judge people . . . " She trailed off and stared into the fire again. Riko squeezed her hand.

"We all do, one way or another. It's just, well, especially as a presidency, we have to judge righteously . . . not faultfinding but looking for the good things." Riko stopped as her gaze fell upon a large antique armoire on the facing wall. She didn't speak for several seconds. "Sharon, where did you get that?" Riko gestured toward the armoire.

"An auction. Up near Leduc." Sharon felt herself smiling for the first time that evening. "Richard thought I was crazy. It looked just awful, Riko. You wouldn't believe it! I think it had been stored in a barn or something. It had about four coats of paint on it, and the handles had all fallen off. See that cornice at the top? It was broken almost all the way through. I glued it and clamped it. You can't tell now unless you look really closely. See?" Sharon pointed to the top of the armoire. "You know, it cost us hardly anything. Of course, I had to put a lot of work into it." Sharon motioned to the low table in front of them. "I got this at the same place. It wasn't in quite as bad a shape, even though I think it's much older. When you look underneath, you can see the old kind of nails in it, with the square heads. Look at this carving, down here. Someone put a lot of work into this. I couldn't leave without it—I just had to refinish it and see what it was really meant to look like."

Riko said nothing for a minute. She pushed her heavy hair back and smiled a wide, slow smile. "You saw past the outside," she said warmly. "You saw potential."

"I . . . I guess I did," Sharon stammered. "I did. I do. I love to refinish furniture. I do it a lot now, with Richard gone." Riko looked as if she was about to share a secret.

"Do it with me," Riko suggested.

"Uh, well, sure, if you want . . . "

"I mean, in this Relief Society calling. Look at the sisters, past the old paint and the cracks and the scratches. Look for the carving and the square nails . . . whatever makes the sisters special. I need you to show me, Sharon. You know a lot more than I do about all this." Riko motioned about her, taking in the family portraits, the heart-shaped wreath of dried flowers, the family home evening chart, the restored furniture. "This is all so different for me."

And now Sharon was Relief Society second counselor. Without Richard here to sustain and support her. Without his comforting arm around her shoulder, the arm that she had leaned on so often in the past.

She was going to have to handle a lot, Sharon sighed to herself. She had prayed, of course. And Richard had prayed. Sharon just wished they could have prayed together. If she could only have seen the confirmation on Richard's face, as well as felt it for herself, maybe it would seem more . . . official. It's just that there's always been someone—Daddy, or one of my brothers, or Richard—to confirm things. This time, Sharon had only herself to turn to, and the Lord.

Her solitary prayers had been answered reassuringly. And of course, Riko said Sharon was the right sister for this calling. As much as Sharon wanted to deny it, she knew that Riko was right.

This isn't that bad, Sharon comforted herself. Other husbands have had to go away; other women have coped. She thought of Mary Ann Young, the wife of Brigham Young. In 1839, Mary Ann had just had a baby when her husband left for a mission to England. She and her children were so sick they couldn't even fetch water. She was left with practically nothing, yet she had survived without phoning England every night or Brigham flying back home to Nauvoo every month. Whereas, Sharon told herself, I just had to decide to accept a calling, and then stand up in church and see if everyone thought my decision was right.

Now that the ordeal of sustaining was over, and the meeting was nearing its close, Sharon could recall it with only a small skip of her heart. She was relieved she was no longer standing, sticking up out of the ward like a weed, with everyone staring at her. Or worse, comparing her to the rest of the new presidency, who all stood so confidently.

Bishop Malmgren had intoned her name, "LaBlanche Sharon Rasmussen." Sharon cringed and smiled apologetically as she rose to her feet. LaBlanche! she despaired. Everyone looked at her, their gaze causing perspiration to bead on Sharon's forehead. She smoothed her shawl around her with shaking hands and tried to stand up straight. Rhonda and Riko looked so serene and unruffled.

Then it was Virginia's turn to stand, as the bishop read, "Virginia Camille Thorne, secretary." Sharon sighed. A *real* name.

Sharon could not look up when the bishop asked if any were opposed. Suppose there were? she thought nervously. To her very great relief, there was no hue and cry against her role in the presidency.

A lump of coal among the diamonds, Sharon ruefully summed herself up. She then sat down once more to the comforting presence of a daughter on either side, breathing a sigh of relief.

Riko was now bearing her testimony. Sharon gathered her shawl in front of her throat, glancing at her watch. The meeting was almost over. She should be listening to Riko's testimony, not feeling sorry for herself, she thought guiltily.

Janie and Megan were on either side of Sharon, leaning their pale blonde heads on their mother's chest, wiggling their warm, bony little frames as tight against her as they could. "You smell pretty, Mommy," complimented Janie in her breathy voice. She patted her mother's cheek, and the two of them shared a warm smile. Sweet Janie! Sharon resolved, yet again, not to compare herself to anyone else, any more.

She tried to focus on Riko's words but, despite her intentions, her thoughts wandered from the testimony.

Richard would not be home for another week. A week mightn't be so awful, Sharon tried to convince herself. She had plenty of things to do in the evenings, that was for sure. She imagined herself in the living room with her needlepoint in her lap, working to the hum of the fridge and the sounds of the children stirring slightly as they drifted to sleep. And there would be a presidency meeting, maybe at Sharon's own house so she wouldn't have to leave the children. She would fill the week somehow. She could hardly wait until church was over to phone Richard and talk to him about her new calling again. Only a week, she soothed herself. Just another week, and he'll be home.

"Andrew!" she whispered, leaning across Sarah's lap to tap her son's knee. "You'll see your friends in Primary. Turn around and pay attention, please." Andrew jerked back around and gave his mother a strange smile. His eyes sparkled merrily with suppressed mischief. Andrew was an irrepressible boy, always the first to see the humor in a situation, bursting with good-natured jokes or lighthearted teasing at his sisters' expense. Well, he'll get a chance to share the joke with his friend soon, Sharon sighed. She hoped he would at least try to be reverent for his Primary teacher. He gets it from Richard, I suppose.

Thirteen-year-old Sarah suddenly whirled her head around and back and then bent over, stifling a giggle. That struck Andrew anew. He broke into one of his broad, unreserved grins, and his shoulders began to shake.

Sharon was mortified. What would people think? She whispered hoarsely, "You two! What would Daddy say if he knew you were behaving like this in church?" Apparently it was the wrong thing to say. It only served to send them into further paroxysms of suppressed snickers.

Riko's testimony drew to a close, the congregation echoing her humble amen. Bishop Malmgren stood to close the meeting. Exasperated, Sharon put an arm around each of the girls. I come to testimony meeting to get spiritual nourishment, and my kids make a spectacle of themselves!

Janie and Megan were wriggling and smiling. Probably some kind of silly, little-girl thing, Sharon thought. The girls' laughing eyes called to each other over the small hands they'd clapped over their mouths, mirth escaping them in soft snorts and puffs. The girls acted like characters from their favorite TV show, who had seen something hysterically funny.

Sharon's face grew very hot. She would be glad when this meeting was ended and she could turn the children over to the Primary. Everyone was probably watching her undisciplined family, she thought, wondering why Riko had asked Sharon Rasmussen to be a counselor when she couldn't even control her own children.

"Girls, sit still now," Sharon tried to calm them. "Sit and think about the nice pictures you're going to draw today to mail to Daddy. Are you going to make a princess, Janie?"

The girls would not take this bait. It seemed Sharon's every attempt to quiet them pushed them further into irreverence. As soon as they caught each other's glances, they were off again. What has gotten into them today? Sharon wondered.

People sitting around them were whispering to one another, pointing. Sharon was sure she knew what they were saying. That Richard's absence was not helping the children any. That she should control them better. Sharon struggled to appear serene.

As Riko again stepped forward, this time to the music stand, Sharon reached for her hymnbook. How I wish I had her poise! Sharon thought once more. Riko lifted her arms, preparing for the rhythmic half-dance of the chorister. Sharon wondered for perhaps the tenth time that day how she could possibly hold a candle to Riko and to Rhonda as a counselor. She opened the green book and flipped through the pages.

The closing hymn was one of her favorites. Familiar notes

surrounded her like welcome arms. Sharon lifted her light soprano voice and felt the Spirit's gentle touch.

"God be with you till we meet again; / By his counsels guide, uphold you . . . "

A man behind her had a voice very like Richard's. Warm and rich, with a comforting sort of sound . . . Just like Richard's . . .

It couldn't be Richard, she chided herself. He was thousands of miles away. It was not Richard. Sharon told herself she missed her husband so much that her mind was playing tricks on her. Still, he sounded so much like Richard . . . Sharon was determined that she would not get excited and make an idiot of herself. It's not Richard, not Richard, not Richard. Sharon chanted the strange mantra in her mind, trying to deflate the balloon of excitement that was swelling within her, pumped by every pounding heartbeat. If she weren't careful, Sharon thought, any moment now the balloon could burst with joy. Or despair. Not Richard, she reminded herself. Not Richard.

She had to look. She had to. Calm, Sharon told herself. Stay calm. After all, it's not Richard. Sharon's throat tightened, her hands clutched at the hymnbook as she strove to appear uninterested. She swallowed hard and turned slowly, pretending to look for someone near the door. Not Richard, she fervently reaffirmed. Not . . .

. . . Richard! All thoughts of composure flew from Sharon like startled sparrows. The hymnbook dropped to the bench. Her eyes grew wide with incredulity, amazement, and tears. How . . . ? He had come home early! Richard grinned, his eyes crinkling in delight at her reaction.

Free at last to give vent to their excitement, the children beamed widely at her slowness to discover their special secret. The members sitting near Richard were all smiling. They had not been saying awful things about her, then! A smile sprang to Sharon's face and would not leave it. She began to sing once more, the notes high and quavering. Richard, grinning, sang the bass notes of the harmony, his voice a caress.

"Are you surprised, Mommy? Are you surprised?" Sharon looked down into Janie's shining face.

Sharon lifted her gaze once more to Richard's. Their eyes locked, tears in both pairs. Sharon hugged Janie to her tightly and whispered, "I have never ceased to be surprised, Janie. I never will." An eternity of love shone from Richard's eyes. With a last, lingering look, Sharon turned back toward the front and picked up the open hymnbook. Her voice rose in joyous song once more.

SISTER BIRD:
CHOKECHERRY JELLY

Esther Bird shifted on the pew. Her left hip, the one she had broken several years ago, sent a sharp needle of pain into her leg. It had become increasingly difficult to sit through her meetings in the last year. Arthritis had laid its bony and tenacious hand upon her slight frame.

Wincing, Esther ran her gnarled hands over the folds of her skirt, remembering with chagrin her humiliation during the sacrament. She had taken a tiny clear cup of water from the tray in front of her and then held up a shaking hand to pass the tray on. Evidently, however, the deacon and Sister Stone had decided she was unfit even for that small duty. Sister Stone's capable hand darted in front of her daughter and Sister Bird and grasped the handle firmly. The tray moved on, without help from either of them. Chastened, Esther Bird bowed her head forward once more to hide her emotions.

Something tickled her memory. She had been thinking of something before that, something important. What was it? She attempted to gather her thoughts, like drifting feathers from a broken pillow. They fluttered in shafts of sunlight and shadow in her mind as she chased them feebly.

Oh yes. She remembered now, with gentle sorrow. Tomorrow would be the sixty-fifth wedding anniversary of Albert and Esther Bird. Her twenty-first without Albert. Years of living in seniors' apartments with the photos and a television and Meals on Wheels. He had been gone a long, a very long time. Yet the ache always remained, small but constant, like the stiffness in her hands.

She absently rubbed her swollen knuckles. The ring would never come off now. She saw Albert, the gilded autumn hills of Longview behind him, the Indian summer sun painting a halo on his dark hair and catching the light of a single diamond. His hand shook as he held the delicate ring between his big fingers. "I want to do it proper, Esther. Want to be with you forever."

Behind Esther, children squirmed and whispered, their parents alternately restless and attentive. That Japanese girl, her visiting teacher, was up at the front bearing her testimony. What was her name again? Nice girl. Kind. She was smiling at her. Esther did her best to smile. Again she sifted through the dancing feathers, looking for the one, the fluffy white one that eluded her grasp.

She had it now. The Alberta Temple. Albert was kneeling across from her, holding her hands tenderly, looking into her face. How fine he was! He made a handsome figure with his dark hair and eyes in the brilliant white clothes. Even in winter he was tanned from working on the ranch. His eyes . . . sometimes it was hard to see the pupils in their depths, they were so dark. On this day, they shone with love and happiness as he knelt across from her in the sealing room. It seemed he was about to speak . . .

"Sister Bird, do your teeth come out?"

The voice was high and small, beside her right ear. Esther opened her eyes, puzzled, and stared hard at the child sitting there. It took her a moment to place her. It was Alison Stone. Her mother insisted on Esther's sitting with their family every week. Alison was about eight or nine years old. A busy child, somewhat bold, but a good girl. She asked a lot of questions. Esther liked her. They had become friends. Esther was far more willing to tolerate the girl's questions than her mother's pity.

"Alison! Don't you bother Sister Bird." Sister Stone fixed an angry and embarrassed glare on her daughter. "I'm sorry," the woman murmured almost inaudibly as she turned away. "Alison, please read your scriptures."

Esther ruminated as the mortified woman bowed her head and shut her eyes. The girl beside her put a blue Book of Mormon on her lap, but did not open it. She glanced up at the old woman from the corner of her eye. "Sorry," she whispered, her voice just on the quavering edge of a sob. Alison stared at her hands.

"Yes. I should think so." Esther Bird's stern voice belied the softness in her face. After a while she added mischievously, "And the answer is yes. They do."

The girl's face popped up like a spring crocus, lit with a grin. "I thought so!" she whispered triumphantly. "Neat!"

"Yes," Esther replied. "Amazing. The Amazing Esther Bird and Her Removable Teeth." She pointed to the book on Alison's lap. "You reading that?" They conversed in hushed tones.

"Well, kind of. I'm almost to Mosiah. But it's taking an awful long time. It's boring."

Two sparse tufts of gray shot up above Esther's glasses. This child was not only bold but misguided. Esther decided to set her straight. "Hmmf. Boring. You think a coupla boys fixing to throw their brother into the sea's boring? Think some young missionary whacking off arms is boring? I hate to think about what life at your house is like."

Esther noticed an angry and incredulous look from Alison's mother but decided not to let on. "You read some more there and then tell me about it. Go on."

The child sighed. "Okay, I will." She grinned impishly, obviously suddenly inspired. "But you have to take out your teeth! Deal?"

Esther sat back to contemplate the proposal. Her left hip sent her a telegraph again. Her knees and shoulders signaled painfully, unwilling to let her forget their existence for even a moment. And her dentures never had been a comfortable fit. "Deal." She slowly dug a tissue from the sleeve of her old blue cardigan and opened it out carefully. Then, with difficulty, she lifted it to her mouth. Very slowly she bent forward. Her tongue found the detestable things and pushed. Quietly, stealthily, she deposited the gleaming teeth into the tissue. She lowered her hand again and then opened it slowly, showing Alison the object of her desire.

Alison's face clearly told Esther that she had never experienced anything as rapturously exciting as this. It was clear by her mother's face that she never had, either. Esther pretended not to see Sister Stone. The girl stared first at the dentures and then at the smiling, toothless old woman next to her. Esther pointed to the book and nodded. Alison bent to fulfill her part of the bargain.

In the symphony of pain attending Esther's tired body, she noticed an unfamiliar, low note. As the girl pored over her reading, occasionally glancing sidelong at her friend, Sister Bird tried to place this new feeling. She mentally probed her aching body. The hip was bad, very bad today. The knees and shoulders were about the same, maybe worse. They keened their discomfort in high, sharp notes. Her misshapen hands throbbed in their twisted poses. But this was deeper and sustained. It moved through her whole body, escalating the nuances in every part. It began . . . where did it begin? Her chest. Yes, her chest. It was as if someone were hugging her tightly. Much too tightly. It was hard to breathe. She closed her eyes and concentrated on her lungs, filling and emptying them.

Her face tensed. Another feather of memory caught the light. Albert was holding her tightly, tightly, rocking her. Her arms were pinned against him. "No!" she screamed, "not my baby! He is going to graduate next month. He is going on a mission!"

Albert's voice was choked with his own sorrow. "Don't cry, honey. It'll be all right. Tommy has a mission there. He's working for Heavenly Father now. No more swathers or balers . . . He's a special kind of missionary now. We always wanted that for him."

"Not like this, Albert! Not like this! Your children aren't supposed to die before you! Our only one, our only one! How could he be taken this way!" She sobbed into Albert's soft chambray shirt. His arms were around her, warming her, holding her, shielding her.

With a shuddering gasp, Sister Bird opened her blue eyes.

It had become even harder than before to breathe. Trills of pain ran up her aching legs, through the twisted fingers and over her hunched shoulders. Exquisite melodies of torment played themselves out in her left hip as she silently prayed. Please, dear Father! Please help me bear it! Esther's twisted fingers gripped the tissue and its contents. She dabbed at her moist forehead.

Finally the pain in her chest began to ease slightly. Esther was able once more to summon all of the strength of her aging lungs to pull life from the air about her. Awakened now, the songs in her bones would not stop or even slow down. They gripped her small frame in dizzying crescendos. The old woman groaned.

Alison's worried face was peering into hers. "Are you all right? You don't look too good," she whispered. "Sister Bird?"

But Sister Bird could not hear her. She was listening to Albert. "You're the prettiest gal in the foothills, Esther. Why'd you ever marry an old dog like me? Now don't cry, Honey. You know I can't stand to see you cry. I'll be back for you, I promise. I told you I'd never leave you." His wrinkled, spotted hands stroked hers. "Give me a kiss now, Esther. I'm gonna miss you." She leaned forward and kissed his mouth, his weathered cheeks, the lines of his forehead. She stroked his thin gray hair. And then he left. She knew when it happened, for his face was suddenly still and somehow different. He was gone.

"Sister Bird," Alison was whispering. She held one of the crepey, blue-veined hands in her own small, smooth ones. "You're right, it's not boring, the book. Well, at least some of it's not. King Benjamin built this huge tower to talk to everyone. How do you think they heard him from way up there? They didn't have microphones. Sister Bird?" The girl's face looked stricken and pale as she realized she could not distract Sister Bird from her pain this time. "Should I tell Mom?"

The wrinkled lips contracted with difficulty. The reply was inaudible, but Sister Bird shook her head slightly. She placed her other hand on top of Alison's and tried to smile reassuringly.

Her chest and throat ached fiercely as she stood by the freshly tamped earth. The headstone read "Albert Edward Bird, Beloved Husband." Tommy and Albert both lay under the Longview pines. They had left her, left her all alone . . . Esther's chest was being crushed with the ache of her abandonment. There was no room inside her for air now.

Incongruously, it reminded her of squeezing the juice from a cheesecloth bag. Tighter, tighter, to make good chokecherry jelly, Albert's favorite. Tighter.

He was calling her, softly and clearly. She could hear him over the agonizing music of her bones and muscles. She could hear him even over the organ. "God be with you till we meet again . . . " they sang.

Esther Bird stood up. He was calling her, and she must go now. She suddenly felt better than she had in years. The pain had stopped. All around her the congregation sang, joined by other, heavenly voices. She looked down at the woman below her, the old one that the girl was talking to. Her hair was very thin on top. My, that was sad. And how disgraceful! There, in her lap, were her teeth. Oh my! That will never do. The child held the old woman's pale hand to her cheek.

"Good-bye." Although Alison whispered, Esther heard her clearly above the beautiful singing. Alison slipped the tissue-wrapped teeth into Esther's open purse. Well, that's a mercy, Esther thought. Dear child. You dear, dear child.

"Esther," he called again. She turned to him. Albert reached out to her, looking handsome and fine in his temple clothes. "I've missed you, honey. I've missed you so much."

EMPTY PACKET AT THE MORTUARY

The car heater blew full blast, the only noise audible over the thrumming engine. Above, the iron sky threatened more snow, wads of dull cloud covering the stars. The four women in the vehicle had chatted sporadically for the past half hour, but now they rode in silence through the darkening streets. Riko drove slowly onward. She was in no hurry to reach their destination. There, the presidency must witness firsthand the inevitable indignity of death and soften its harsh ravaging.

Bishop Malmgren had explained last night as he and Riko talked in his office. "She left a letter for me." He held up a worn missive, his voice gentle. "She left one for you too, Riko." He handed it to her, a plain envelope yellowed and softened about the corners from contact with Esther Bird's life. Riko's shaking hand accepted it.

She read the words written in crabbed, pointed handwriting: "To the Relief Society President of My Ward, in the Event of My Death." Its date revealed that it had been written a few years ago. It was a humble request from Sister Bird that the sisters of the Relief Society presidency dress her body for her funeral.

Riko's eyes had filled with tears: tears for Sister Bird, for her touching trust in an unknown sister, and angry tears for herself. A body—preparing a body for burial! she wailed silently. She recalled the face of death worn by her grandmother. Riko had found her that awful day several months ago, pale and gray in the bed she had slept in for more than forty years. Grandma's eyes were glazed, not quite closed. Her hands, the tools of so much creativity, had become rigid claws. "I can't do it." Riko shook her head. "It is too awful!" She sat down.

Bishop Malmgren sat beside her. "I know you've never done anything like this, Riko, but you will be blessed. You'll see." Riko tried to believe him, but she was distraught at the responsibility that had fallen into her lap so soon after her setting apart. The bishop murmured reassuringly for a few minutes and then produced a card from his breast pocket. "Here's the number of Brother Dorcas at the funeral home, Riko. He's a very understanding, compassionate man. He will prepare her for you, and his wife will wash her—you won't need to do that." The bishop paused. "Brother Dorcas will tell you everything you need to know."

Everything, Riko thought as she spotted the mortuary ahead, except how to look at an old, dead woman and not feel sick. Why, she wondered, couldn't Sister Dorcas dress the body as well as wash it? She answered herself resignedly, Because Sister Bird doesn't want a stranger to make her look like someone else. And, she admitted, it would be nice to know a friend was dressing you once you had died. The last word seemed to drop into Riko's brain like a stone down a dark shaft. *Died.*

In the passenger seat beside Riko, Rhonda stared out the window. Behind them sat Sharon and Virginia. Sharon's head was bowed, her hands covering her face. The garish lights of a convenience store played across Virginia's doll-like features. None of them, Riko sighed, was comfortable with this aspect of their calling.

Riko's glance slid sideways. Rhonda sat in the passenger side of the front seat, unmoving, her eyes listlessly reading the words that floated by: Adult Video Superstore . . . Buy 'N Sell Discount Furniture . . . Chez Jackie Hair Affair . . .

The funeral home had been in a flourishing district once, on a major artery to Calgary's downtown. Now it was surrounded by gas stations, pawn shops, and strip malls, service outlets for those who lived in the mobile homes, aging houses, and dimly lit apartment buildings nearby.

Riko focused her thoughts once more on the traffic. Rhonda's voice, with its trace of humor, broke the silence. "Unreal, isn't it? I can't quite believe we're doing this." She and Riko exchanged a glance. Riko wondered if Rhonda saw the fear in her eyes or the tremble of her hand as she reached to switch down the heater.

"It was her request, after all," Riko managed. "She didn't want a stranger to do it. I guess she wanted to look just right for . . ."

Riko did not finish her sentence. She tried to picture Sister Bird without life but instead saw her grandmother's ashen face once more. She shivered. I hope Sister Bird doesn't look like that, she thought. Please, Heavenly Father, help me to see her without revulsion. Help me to be strong.

They turned into the parking lot past a large sign, painted to resemble stained glass. "The Dorcas Funeral Chapel," script lettering announced solemnly.

Riko pulled the car underneath the peach glow of a sodium light, as far as possible from the lurking hearses. She looked at her companions. In the eerie light they seemed stone-faced and drawn.

"Well," Riko nodded, "this is it." The women unfolded themselves from Riko's small car. They clustered around the trunk, shouldering their purses, as Riko carefully removed Sister Bird's garment bag and folded it over one arm.

"Customer Parking Only," Rhonda pointed to the sign. "How many of their customers drive themselves here, do you think?" Her feeble attempt to leaven the situation was met with self-conscious smiles. The sisters began to pick their way across the icy parking lot. It was liberally sprinkled with sand, and they hadn't much chance of losing their footing. Still, the four women held on to one another, glad to have an excuse to do so. Riko opened the heavy glass door to the lobby of the Dorcas Funeral Home.

Brother Dorcas took care of all the Latter-day Saint funerals in the city, as had his father before him. He was a brawny man, tanned even in midwinter. His thin, fair hair framed a round face with a ready smile and blue eyes. He reached a hand toward Riko as the women entered the foyer. "Ah, you must be Sister Ikuta. Welcome, sisters. Let me take your coats." He hung them in a fragrant closet behind oak doors. "Would you like to gather your thoughts for a moment, before I take you to see her?" He paused, questioningly. "No? Well, then, if you'll just follow me . . ." Brother Dorcas gestured toward a hallway, pale blue and gold, that led to a large wooden door. The women walked hesitantly upon the thick carpet, none of them anxious to be the first to reach the door. Brother Dorcas squeezed past them and turned the brass knob. In the room beyond, Riko glimpsed a long table and a white-shrouded form.

"Wait!" Riko's own voice sounded high and odd to her. "I

mean, if you don't mind, Brother Dorcas . . . I think we should have a prayer first."

"Yes," Rhonda's slender hand flew to her throat. "Of course." The other women nodded.

Brother Dorcas smiled. "Why don't I show you into one of our meditation rooms." He opened one of the wooden doors. "You can take all the time you'd like. Just give me a knock here," he motioned to a door opposite, "when you're ready." He showed them in and softly closed the door.

The women entered with a sense of relief, finding places to sit in the elegant armchairs and on the French Provincial sofa. As if by one accord they folded their arms and sat primly in anticipation of the prayer. The sisters looked at Riko.

Riko hardly trusted herself to speak, afraid she would give voice to the panic that threatened to well up inside her and beg for help—or, better still, reprieve. She cleared her throat. This is my job. This is bigger than I am, and I have to do it, she admonished herself.

She bowed her head, and the others followed suit. Riko forced herself into composure.

"Beloved Father in Heaven . . . " she began. Haltingly, her heart still racing, she asked for serenity and sisterhood to attend the four women as they performed their duties. She paused. The women seemed to be holding their breath. Riko whispered, "And please help us to work well together and to lift one another."

The amen was a collective sigh, regretful yet resigned, the sigh of Eve, of Martha, of Woman, stolidly facing the frayed and crumbling evidence of mortality and its duties.

Riko reached out and took Sharon's and Virginia's cool hands, as did Rhonda. Every eye was downcast.

Riko squeezed their hands lightly. "Let's go." She managed

to sound more confident than she felt. She crossed the hallway and tapped on Brother Dorcas's door. He appeared, again ushering them toward their duty. "You understand what is required?" Riko nodded mutely. "Well, I don't want to intrude. I'll just leave you to it." Brother Dorcas opened the door and motioned the presidency into the large room. Riko stepped inside gingerly. The other women followed her, footsteps echoing on the tile. "Just come get me if you need anything at all." The doorway was filled with his broad shoulders for a moment, and he retreated from the room. The sisters looked around.

This room was spacious and dimly lit, except for a lamp that hung from the high ceiling, throwing its light in a wide circle over the center of the room. Beneath it stood a waist-high metal table, draped in a sheet. Under this shroud, a figure lay supine— a figure, Riko knew, that had once been Esther Bird, the woman regarded as the Ward Grandma. The women approached cautiously, setting their purses on the floor and the garment bag on a nearby chair.

For several moments they stood gazing at the shrouded body in front of them. Riko became aware of the faint buzz of the light fixture, the barely audible music piped in through unseen speakers. Before them loomed the table and its gleaming snowdrift, reminding Riko incongruously of the sacrament table.

At last Riko walked to one end of the table and took hold of the sheet covering the body. She gestured to Sharon, across from her, to take a corner as well. Startled, Sharon started to back away but then set her mouth and met Riko's eyes with a calm green glance. Slowly, very slowly, the two women folded back the white covering to the shoulders of the corpse.

The only one of them to make a sound was Virginia, who gasped slightly and quickly covered her mouth.

Sister Bird was not Sister Bird. She was a wax figure, a carica-
ture of the old woman whom so many in the ward had loved. The
body that lay before them was gray and unnatural. Naked and
unconcerned, it looked as if it could never have held a spirit as
warm and expressive as Esther Bird's. Riko forced herself to look,
shoving away the horror that crept about the calm center of her
mind trying to find a way in.

This is not Grandma. This is Sister Bird, and she needs us
now, she thought forcefully as she studied the wrinkled face
before them. Sister Bird's eyes were closed, without the deep fur-
row between them that had marked her last, painful grimace.
Dark circles touched the eyes and hollowed the cheeks. Deep
seams ran from the nose to the corner of the lined mouth.
Brother Dorcas's careful work had restored the mouth to a normal
fullness, Riko noted. On that terrifying day in the chapel it had
sunk and shriveled without its inner frame of dentures.

Bordered by the folded sheet, thin shoulders framed a collarbone. It lay beneath the skin like the wooden bones of old furniture under a carelessly tossed apron. Riko remembered Grandma
in her bed: not sleeping, still and dead.

Riko felt her will recoiling and turned away. The others stood
watching. No one spoke for a few seconds. Riko sighed, her
shoulders drooping.

A soft voice spoke. "This is the last thing anyone can do for
her here, sisters—the last service we can perform." Riko looked
up in astonishment. Sharon laid a hand upon the old woman's
head and stroked it gently. "Maybe she'll thank us someday."
Riko stared at this reclusive woman before her, bending over a
corpse with a look of tenderness and pity as if her generous
thoughts alone would assure Sister Bird of exaltation. She had
echoed Sister Bird's own words.

Riko hesitated. "You're right, Sharon. Look, I have something to read to you all, from Sister Bird." Riko pulled the worn
envelope from her purse. "Listen to this," she said, and began to
read.

"Dear Sister ? :

*"As I have no living family, it falls to you to ready me for my
funeral. As my mother always said, 'A pretty bride is easily dressed!' I
hope your task is not a difficult one. I have prepared the clothing in a
garment bag that you will find in the hall closet. I hope I have not forgotten anything.*

*"I rest knowing you will know what to do and will make every-
thing right for me. You know how I should look. It is a comfort to me to
have the loving hands of sisters perform this final service. I am very
grateful to you and your presidency. I hope to thank you all, face to
face, someday.*

"Sincerely,
"Esther L. Bird

*"P.S. Please make sure I am wearing my gold locket with the pic-
tures in it. You will find it on my bureau in a velvet box. There is
makeup and a hairbrush also. Yours, E.L.B."*

Riko looked up. Every eye was moist. It was as if, hearing the
words of the woman whose body lay lifeless in their midst, they
saw her full of life again. She was no longer just a body. She was
Esther Bird, their sister. She had reached out to them and
requested their help, and they were honored to perform this final
service.

Riko knew by Rhonda's calm smile that she, too, could feel

that warmth. Sharon was gazing compassionately at the still face of Sister Bird. Virginia's eyes were closed tightly, her face tense.

Riko reached for the bag near her feet and began to place snowy undergarments, still in their plastic packages, on the sheet before her. "We should put these on her first, under the sheet. Then, when she's covered, we can take the sheet off and do the rest." Sharon and Rhonda nodded assent.

Sharon cradled the gray head reverently, as Riko and Rhonda gently slipped the chemise over Sister Bird's head and down over her shoulders. They slid Sister Bird's thin arms through the short sleeves with little difficulty, and slipped the garment downward, smoothing it lightly. Replacing the sheet over her chest again, tenderly, they moved to the other end of the table. As if their motions had been choreographed, the two women slid the under-clothing up under the sheet and over Sister Bird's gnarled feet and along her legs, snugging the garment about her waist.

Riko took the large bag from the back of the chair. The zip-per hummed as she opened it, and white fabric gleamed dully from inside. Virginia, glad to find herself a task, rushed to Riko's side. "Here, let me," she offered, and she drew the temple dress from the bag. "It's beautiful!" Virginia whispered, and indeed it was. The dress was long, simple in design, and sewn meticulously of soft, satinlike material. The fabric hung in gentle folds from the waist, and delicate embroidery chased about the collar and wrists. "It looks as if it's never been worn."

"Maybe she had it made for this," Riko suggested. "She must have known for a while that she was going to . . . "

"Look!" Virginia breathed. "The slippers!" The white slippers were dainty, beaded with small faux pearls and adorned with tiny bows. They were still in their original factory box. In a separate cloth packet, neatly folded, waited Sister Bird's temple clothes.

"What's in there?" Rhonda gestured to a blue-green over-
night case on the floor. Virginia pushed the clasps, and they
flipped open. She lifted the lid. The case contained a small makeup bag and a hairbrush, hair spray, and some hairpins. There was
a new brassiere, an unopened package of white hose, and a small
red velvet box. Virginia opened it. "That looks like real gold,"
she remarked, as she withdrew a small locket.

Rhonda looked thoughtful. "I wonder . . . would she mind
if we opened it?" They looked at Riko questioningly.

"I . . . I don't think she'd mind. She was the kind of person who told you everything." They shared a smile as they
remembered Esther Bird's sometimes startling honesty. Virginia
opened the locket with a long pink thumbnail. Two tiny black-
and-white pictures looked up at the sisters. One was of a middle-
aged man, dark-haired and handsome, smiling broadly. The other
was of a boy, his light hair blowing about his face, looking as if
he were about to run off. "Her husband and son, I think," Riko
said quietly.

Rhonda spoke. "Her son died young. Car accident?" she
asked.

"Sister Bird didn't talk about it much. I gather it was pretty
grisly." Riko paused. "It was harvest, and Tommy had gone to
help a neighbor. He got caught in the swather. I think it took his
arm. He lost a lot of blood right away."

The sisters were listening intently. Riko looked at the picture
of Esther Bird's husband. "When Albert got there, Esther was
clinging to Tommy's body, crying and carrying on. She was all
covered with blood. He pulled her away and put her in the truck.
Then he put Tommy in the back. After he put Esther to bed and
got Tommy all cleaned up, he went into the barn and stood there,

in the dark, covered in dirt and blood. Stood there and yelled at the rafters." Riko stopped.

"Albert died a few years later."

The women pondered silently for several seconds and then straightened up as Virginia closed the locket. Sharon again cradled the head as Virginia slid the thin chain around Sister Bird's neck and fastened the clasp with shaking hands. "There," she said, arranging the locket on the old woman's bony chest. "That's better."

"You know," Sharon began, "Sister Bird was my visiting teacher, years ago when we first moved into the ward." Riko began rummaging through the small flowered bag, finding make-up base. Sharon continued. "One day she came over with Sister Pilling. It was summer, and it was pretty warm in the house. She was sitting right by the window, you know, Riko? On the sofa. Anyway, she was right in the sun, and her partner was talking, giving me the lesson. And Sister Bird sort of . . . well, she fell asleep!"

The other women looked at Sharon in surprise, their smiles encouraging her to go on. "We sat there for a while, making conversation, but finally the sisters had to go." Sharon beamed at Sister Bird, who was now being daubed with foundation by Riko.

"Finally, we got my daughter Sarah to come into the living room. She was only about four or five, and Sister Bird always fussed over her. Anyway, we asked Sarah to sing that song, 'Once there was a snowman, snowman . . . ' You know, from Primary? We told her, 'Sarah, Sister Bird would love to hear you sing, real loud.' So Sarah sang it, and . . . nothing. Sister Bird kept sleeping.

" 'Sarah, sing it again, in your loudest voice, because Sister Bird can't hear very well,' we said. So Sarah just pipes up, 'Once there was a SNOWMAN . . . ' " Sharon giggled. "And then

poor old Sister Bird. She opens her eyes as if nothing's happened
and says, 'Why, Miss Doris Day! Could I please have your auto-
graph, ma'am?' She was such a sweetheart!"

The women all chuckled. Riko felt her fingers relax a little
bit as she continued to apply the foundation to Sister Bird's face,
carefully trying to create a smooth finish. It wasn't working. She
stopped, the sponge in midair.

"She always kind of reminded me of my grandma," Riko said,
smiling. "She was just always . . . all right with whatever was
happening. I got to visit teach her a few times. Her apartment is
stuffed with pictures and books and plants." Riko's smile deepened. "She wanted to make everyone comfortable in her home.
And she really did."

Rhonda spoke up. "Remember that time in Relief Society
when they asked for sisters to collect things for the women's shelter? No one expected Sister Bird to do much—she was so old. But
the next week she phoned the Relief Society president and asked
her to come and pick up 'a few things.' A few things turned out to
be six big boxes of clothing and an envelope of money that she'd
collected from the other people in her building!"

The women worked as they spoke, Sharon sliding the knee-
high hose onto the pale legs, Rhonda brushing Sister Bird's hair
this way and that, trying to make it look right, and Riko once
again applying foundation. Only Virginia stood watching, uncertainly shifting from foot to foot in her high-heeled boots, her
arms crossed tightly across her chest.

"She crocheted blankets for me when Jessica Rose and
Ashleigh Anne were born," Virginia said at last. "It must have
taken her hours." She glanced at a knotted hand lying on top of
the sheet. "And it must have been hard for her, with her arthritis."

They were all smiling now, trading stories of the Ward

Grandma as her body lay before them being prepared for the final ordinance of earthly life.

"Remember when she told us that story about the garter snakes getting into the church out in Mountain View and swaying to the organ music?" The sisters burst out laughing, remembering the story that Sister Bird had maintained was absolutely true.

Virginia walked over to Riko and touched her on the arm. "She needs a bit of lavender corrector beneath that, so she won't look sallow. Hold on, I've got some." Riko's eyes widened with surprise as Virginia opened her large, expensive handbag and found the small tube. "This should do it. Just a bit—you won't even see it when it's finished."

"Right," said Riko. "Yellow and purple are complementary colors. Of course!" She began to apply the contents of the tube sparingly.

"Rhonda," Virginia asked, "would you mind if I did that? I have an idea."

"By all means." Rhonda handed Virginia the hairbrush. Rhonda and Riko exchanged a surprised glance as Virginia began to smooth the gray tufts into waves about the now rosier face.

Riko skillfully applied the rouge to Sister Bird's sunken cheeks. With a small brush she outlined the seamed lips carefully and applied lipstick. "It takes a steady hand to do that," Virginia remarked. "How do you do it?"

"Practice," Riko replied. "Long hours at the College of Art." She painstakingly applied mascara and a thin line of eye pencil. "What do you think? Should she have eyeshadow?"

The women studied Sister Bird judiciously. Virginia nodded. "Yes," said Rhonda. "Just a bit in the crease. May I?"

When she was finished, Virginia said, "She looks like Sister Bird again, ready for a special occasion."

"Which," Sharon said, "she is. I think she looks great."

Riko folded the sheet and placed it on the chair. "Now, the dress." The four women all worked at easing the arms into the sleeves and gently tugging the dress down over Sister Bird's body. Virginia and Sharon put a dainty slipper over each foot. Riko buttoned the bodice of the white dress and pulled the locket from inside the neckline to rest upon it. Rhonda smoothed the hair carefully about Sister Bird's peaceful face and buttoned the embroidered cuffs about her bony wrists. Then, in silence, came the temple clothing: the sheer robe that lay about her like a cloud, the green satin apron covered in leafy embroidery, the sash tied about her waist. The sisters worked without speaking, keenly aware of the honor that had befallen them with this duty. At last they placed the veil upon her head, gently folding it beneath her. They stood back and assessed their work.

Sister Bird lay in a pool of light that seemed to shine from her temple dress and ignite a spark on the locket on her chest. Surrounded by a mist of white chiffon, her face was soft with the stillness of peace. She was beautiful.

Her gnarled hands lay on her chest, the left one on top with its small gleaming wedding band. The dress beneath the sheer robe flowed downward like cream, edged in lace, with two small slippers protruding from the hem. The verdant green of the apron gleamed richly.

"I think she would be pleased," Riko stated simply.

"I'm sure she is," Sharon said emphatically. They all smiled.

"She was quite a woman, our Sister Bird," said Rhonda.

Riko raised her arms, drawing the sisters into a hug that lasted for several seconds. She was hugged in return, and then they straightened and prepared to leave Sister Bird until tomorrow.

They left the quiet room with its buzzing lamp, each turning for a final look at the ethereal figure in its center. Sharon, the last one out, paused a moment. "Good-bye," she whispered and closed the heavy oak door behind her.

Sister Bird lay surrounded in light, an eternity away.

EPILOGUE

Riko rolled down the car window. It was almost the official first day of spring, and for once March was a lamb rather than a lion. The hills were still brown, but traces of green were beginning to show. There were only occasional patches of snow high in the foothills, and the air was fresh.

Her hair began to escape the clips she had used to pull it back. Strands looped and danced about her round face as the landscape flowed by. Riko was not sure where she was going today. It was too nice a day to stay indoors. After the brutal cold snap that had been February, everyone, it seemed, had cabin fever.

Heading out of the city toward the mountains on the horizon, she drove past farmhouses, acreages, barns, and stables. Much had happened in the three months since she had driven through these hills to Esther Bird's burial.

The ward was changing. Darla Boynton had been sent to a clinic in the States for treatment. Ruth was alternately hopeful and pessimistic about her daughter's recovery. Andrea Daines's daughter Tara had been baptized. That had seemed to lessen the tension in Andrea's face every Sunday. And the new chorister—Maggie Hartley had reactivated at just the right time.

Riko had attended the Sullivans' sealing at the Alberta Temple. She felt a prickle of goosebumps as she recalled Louise's rapt face gazing into Ethan's during the ceremony.

Rhonda Fitzpatrick and her husband were still teetering on the brink of reconciliation.

"The more things change, the more they remain the same," Riko remembered the old saying.

Glenda Klassen was almost over the nauseous part of her pregnancy and getting to the showing part. First to second trimester, Riko recalled hearing. Glenda's husband wanted another little girl. Esther Jane they would call her, he said.

The sign ahead read, "Longview 15 km." Riko grinned. She knew where she was going now. It was only a few minutes to the town, past the hunkering hills. Longview itself wasn't much to look at—rows of houses receding into the brown grass of the hills, a few gas stations, the post office, a library, several stores strung along the main street. Riko drove slowly until she found the shop she wanted.

A bell tinkled as she pushed open the door. From behind the counter, a face popped up. "Be right with you." Riko nodded and walked to the refrigerated glass case.

Roses stood in stately grace, clustered to themselves. Tulips seemed to fall all over one another welcoming Riko with their profusion of colors. Baby's breath, delicate as lace, filled a large pot. There were daisies and carnations, irises and chrysanthemums and lilies and daffodils.

The graying woman walked to Riko's side. "Made up your mind, dear?"

Riko made her selections. Wrapping the bunch of flowers,

the saleslady smiled. "Lovely spring bouquet. For someone special?"

"For someone very special," Riko agreed. She paid for the flowers, picked them up in their paper cone, and got back into the car. Her destination was just a short drive from town.

Riko pulled over on the narrow gravel road beneath the pine trees. She inhaled their perfume and listened to high, sweet notes of birdsong as she walked to the gravesite.

"Esther Litchfield Bird," read the marker, a long slab of granite that lay across three graves like the headboard of a big bed. "Albert Franklin Bird" was on the opposite end of the pinkish stone. Between those names was carved "Thomas Albert Bird." Sister Bird had joked that she and Albert needed to be buried on either side of their son. "We want to wake him up when the trumpet sounds," she'd said. "Tommy always was a real heavy sleeper." The family circle was complete here at this little plot of ground.

Riko recalled looking through Sister Bird's treasured scriptures. A passage from John had jumped out at her, underlined in red pencil that had been blurred by the repeated tracings of a trembling finger:

"In my Father's house are many mansions: if it were not so, I would have told you. I go to prepare a place for you.

"And if I go and prepare a place for you, I will come again, and receive you unto myself; that where I am, there ye may be also."

She had said that Albert and Tommy were preparing a place, too. That she'd hoped they'd learned to hang things up and keep them neat. Well, she'll know by now, Riko smiled.

She opened the florist's wrapping. In the sculpted granite vase, she placed, first, the daisies. Simple and clean-looking, the bright blossoms reminded her of Sister Bird. This would be *Shin*, heaven. Next was *Soe*, the place of harmony. Riko added the small lily, the carnation, the bunch of tiny violets, and the pink rose. Now *Hakai*, earth. Carefully she arranged the daffodils, multicolored tulips, and baby's breath. Each blossom had a place.

She sat back on her heels. Grandma would approve, though this arrangement was fuller and busier than Grandma's had been. And Sister Bird? Sister Bird would love it. Riko turned her face toward the sun and inhaled the scent of barely-spring.

She stood and brushed the damp earth from her jeans and then headed back toward the car. She took one last look at the three graves under the pines. A robin hopped across the greening grass. Its song rose in liquid notes to the warming air.